A TALE OF TEN WICKETS

The customary novelist's disclaimer may be more necessary than usual: the characters in this book are entirely imaginary and bear no relation to any real person. This novel is about a cricket team rather like the one I play for regularly. In its pages, several members of my team may recognize playing styles, mannerisms, and catch phrases. None, unless by complete coincidence, will recognize their life stories.

Richard Heller, London 1994

RICHARD HELLER

A Tale of Ten Wickets

OVAL PUBLISHING
1994

First published in 1994 by
Oval Publishing
30 Crewdson Road
London SW9 0LJ

ISBN 0-9523419-0-5

Typeset in Century 11/13pt by Scriptmate Editions
Manufacture coordinated in UK by Booksprint
20 Shepherds Hill, London N6 5AH
Printed and bound in Great Britain by
Biddles Ltd, Guildford and King's Lynn

Contents

The Accidental Spectator

In his forty-three years Stephen Devane had woken up in many uncomfortable and outlandish places—a gravestone in Macau, a warehouse in Surabaya, prison cells in Oran, Quito and Belmopan. But it was still a novel sensation to wake up in a scorebox beside a cricket field in the wilds of southern England.

The sun was already high and it was stifling in the airless hut. He opened the door and identified the buzz which had finally woken him as a motor mower, shaving the square of the cricket pitch. He gulped air. He had no idea where he was but he was beginning to remember how he had got there.

The sudden, uncontrollable impulse to see the cottage where he had lived over twenty years ago... a train journey to Franchester ... a walk to Steeple Hawken ... striking out through the Great Wood ... night falling with no sign of the end of the path or human settlement ... the final welcome sight of the open field with the pavilion (locked) and the scorebox (open) ... stretching out on the wooden floor with his camera bag for a pillow...

Stephen remembered all this but it did nothing to relieve the fact that he was hopelessly lost. Since he was a highly successful travel writer, who had walked all over the world, his predicament was distinctly embarrassing. He prepared to seek enlightenment from the man on the mower.

Stephen's books had not yet made him a Household Face, and the man naturally mistook him for a dosser.

'Hoy! What's your game?'

'I'm sorry, is this your hut?' said Stephen foolishly. 'My name is Stephen Devane…' He paused for recognition: none came. 'Here's a card.'

The mower man looked at it, and then took in Stephen's rumpled but fashionable clothes, and relaxed.

'I walked here from Franchester last night.'

The mower man's eyebrows shot up.

'Am I anywhere near Lowden village?'

'We play against them. But that's fifteen miles over the other side of the wood.'

'Fifteen miles? Then where the hell am I?'

'This is Upton Cerney. Here, I don't suppose you'd like a game of cricket, would you?'

'No!' said Stephen, before he remembered his manners. 'I'm sorry, I didn't mean… I really would be hopeless, you have no idea. Look, I'm sorry about sleeping in your hut, but there's nothing broken, and I'd be happy to put something into club funds in exchange for a night's sleep, but first I really would be grateful if you could show me the gents.'

'No harm,' said the mower man. He waved Stephen's money aside and directed him behind a tree. He joined him there and glanced quickly around. The two men emptied their bladders. As an amateur anthropologist, Stephen recognized the signal: he had been accepted into the local tribe.

'Frank Wall's my name,' said the mower man. 'Shame you can't play. We're a man short. We've got a team all the way from London today. The Frenetics. It's hard to get our boys out for a friendly these days. It's not right. They come from London every year, and bring their own scorer, we ought to have a full side. I suppose it'll have to be young Roy…'

Stephen ignored this final unspoken appeal. 'Look, I really would be happy to take photos, and you would be much better off.' To clinch the point he showed off the Pentax and the extension lens.

Frank Wall unlocked the pavilion and performed mystic rituals with a boiler. 'In five minutes there should be enough hot water for a shave and a shower. Here, young Roy!' Stephen noticed a lurking adolescent, wearing Acid House shorts and trainers too large for any conceivable training. 'Do you fancy a game this afternoon?'

'All right.' Stephen smiled: this boy thinks he's too old to be overjoyed.

'Can you get your brother to score? Tell him he can have a video. And will you go to the store and get a toothbrush and a razor for Mr ... er?...' Young Roy shambled off towards the village.

Frank Wall excused himself and applied whiting to the creases of the pitch. He then whacked six stumps into the parched ground. Stephen gulped some more air. Young Roy trotted back with the razor and toothbrush, and Stephen took them into the pavilion. He emerged clean and refreshed, and Frank Wall gave him a brief guided tour of the village.

Upton Cerney got a mention in the Domesday Book. Henry III had a setback there against Simon de Montfort. Several local Robin Hoods used the Great Wood, until finally brought to book by Queen Elizabeth's Justice of the Peace. The Early English church was knocked about a bit by Cromwell and the Victorian rebuilding was a mistake which even Betjeman could not love, but there is a fine surviving Tudor barn. Mr Stanley Baldwin paid Upton Cerney a visit in 1933 and was stirred into one of his famous speeches on the English landscape, but that was before the power station.

The view to the east will never be the same, but the power station provides enough jobs and money to secure the village a cricket team. Its present population is hardworking but tolerant, with a tendency to vote Liberal

Democrat or Green. Its gardens, pets and children are well cared for and its houses still left open at night. The annual pig roast is well attended but the parish council worries about the lack of activities for young people.

Stephen took several photographs before Frank Wall took him to the Bat And Ball pub, pressed a pint into his hands and introduced him awkwardly to some other villagers. Stephen felt himself in the way. After buying a round he returned to the pitch and reconnoitred positions for action photographs. He watched the village team slowly arrive.

Two men already in whites threw catches at each other. Three younger men, still in shorts and mildly obscene T-shirts, attempted Brazilian things with a football. A fourth young man tried to persuade a pretty girl to join him on his motorbike. Young Roy reappeared, in white trousers which had been made to serve one season too many.

Stephen stood in front of the scorebox. He was startled by a peevish cough. 'Would you mind moving when the match starts?'

Stephen looked at the new occupant of the scorebox. He saw a thin man, slightly older than himself. Although his features were nondescript he had a curious air of authority. 'I don't think we've met. I'm the Frenetic scorer. I like to set up here ahead of time.'

Stephen watched him open a large, black artists' portfolio. He extracted two scorebooks, a vast array of coloured pencils, sharpeners and erasers, a ruler, a calculator and a bottle of calligraphic ink. On a new page of one scorebook he entered, in a decorative italic hand, the names of the teams, the ground and the date. 'Weather, Fine and Dry,' he added firmly, with another entry in his beautiful writing.

Frank Wall bustled up. 'Everything all right for you, Mr Scorer? Would you like a pint brought to you?'

'No thank you, Frank. After the match if I may. But I would be most grateful now for a bottle of mineral water. I had some in my car but Pat Hobby's still asleep in the back seat and it would be cruel to wake him.'

Frank Wall headed back to the pub.

'My name is Stephen Devane,' said Stephen and this time he had a reward.

'Not the one who writes those travel books? We are honoured. We had The Road Of Jade as a Book At Bedtime… Quite unsuitable,' he added hastily, 'since it kept everyone awake.'

'Thank you. I am indeed that Stephen Devane.'

'Do you find it easy to write?'

'I suppose so. What about yourself, have you written any books?'

The question seemed to throw the scorer into a tizzy. 'Good lord, no! At least… well, in a manner of speaking … Do these count as books?' He showed Stephen the scorebooks.

'These are beautiful … they're works of art.'

'With these books I could tell you everything that happened in any of our past matches. A different colour pencil for each bowler, so I can tell exactly how many balls each batsman took from each bowler, and that's my own symbol for a missed chance and where it was missed, and there's a run out and who did it…'

'Works of art,' Stephen repeated.

'I haven't introduced myself. Scorer is actually my name. When you heard Frank Wall call me "Mr Scorer" you may have thought it was a title, like Mr President, but it is my name. To make it worse, my first name is Antony. A Scorer. A Scorer by name, a scorer by trade.'

He looked around and continued when he was certain that only Stephen was listening. 'You're a writer. Can you imagine having your whole life shaped by a joke? When I was sent away to prep school the cricket master saw my name and insisted I had to be the scorer. Never asked me if I wanted to play. Actually, I was quite good but he never allowed me to play. So the only way I could get revenge was to become a superb scorer, and when that master was umpiring I would call out from my scorebox and query all his signals, and he would get very flustered and cross but he could do nothing because I was so brilliant at scoring. Then I did the job at public school, and after that I did Minor Counties and MCC and even Ireland versus Scotland.'

'Do you do it for a living?'

'No. You will not be surprised to learn that I am an accountant.'

'There really are works of art,' said Stephen yet again. He wrestled with a question. 'Are the ... Frenetics a very important club?'

'They are to me.'

His tone made Stephen shy away from the question why. Instead he asked 'Why are they called Frenetics?'

'It's a catchphrase of the club captain and founder. "Frightfully grateful if you could help out this weekend, my life's a bit *frenetic* at the moment." Anyway, it stuck.'

Then he answered Stephen's unspoken question. 'When you write your travel books you look for the romance in ordinary things, ordinary people, don't you? That's what's so interesting. I mean, any damn fool can get excited by the Taj Mahal in moonlight, but finding the romance of a railway shed in Calcutta, that's the real wonder... Well, it's the same for me. It's easy to get excited scoring for the MCC or a first-class match, but it's these weekend people, these ... Frenetics ... I find fascinating. I could tell you an unusual story about every one of them.'

'I'll hold you to that.'

By now there was more urgency in the preparations for the match. Frank Wall completed his round-up of the Upton Cerney team. The swain with the motorcycle abandoned his pursuit of the pretty girl and bowled a very fast delivery, fortunately without a ball in his hand. The footballers changed sport and threw spectacular catches at each other. A gray-haired man rehearsed his forward defensive shot. Young Roy tried various settings for the waistband of his white trousers. A man with a red baseball cap and matching face put on some wicketkeeping gloves, and slowly but spontaneously the Upton Cerney players formed a circle around him and began a serious fielding practice.

The Frenetics' preparations were less structured. Stephen watched a convoy of cars manoeuvre for parking space behind the pavilion. The first discharged a small, energetic man who bounded towards the pavilion, and then, as if struck by a sudden remembrance, rushed back to his car and let out his wife, two small daughters, two bicycles, an icebox and a fox terrier.

'Our captain,' said Antony Scorer. The second car was elderly and scarred. It parked ineptly, not helped by the toy tiger which blocked the rear window, and a graying man emerged with an athletic boy about twelve years old. Although they did not look alike, Stephen marked them instantly as father and son. The third car offered a long-haired man who scowled over the scene until a chic woman squeezed his hand.

The next car, a large Mercedes, was opened by a chauffeur. A man on the backseat said 'I want the McGintys *killed*' into a car telephone as he switched off a built-in television. He then swept to the pavilion. Stephen noted his Ray-Ban sunglasses and a real, not Hong Kong, Vuitton holdall. The chauffeur followed with new pads and an unmarked Newbery bat.

Frank Wall returned with mineral water and a smaller and fatter version of Young Roy.

'Now then, Sam. Say how do you do to Mr Scorer, and ask him to help you when you can't keep up.'

Sam looked at Antony's magnum opus and gasped 'Cor! Do I have to do all that?'

'Don't worry. So long as we agree on the score,' Antony reassured him, ominously.

'You can put down nought for my brother. R Gribben. He's useless.'

The conference was interrupted by a tall, shambling figure wearing a formerly beautiful linen suit. 'Oh, Antony, could I have the keys to your boot? It's got my stuff...'

The suit noticed Stephen and broke into an ingratiating smile. 'Pat Hobby.' He paused for recognition, then added 'I'm a writer.'

Antony tossed him the keys. Pat Hobby waved vaguely. 'Gotta change. Pat Hobby,' he repeated and stumbled away.

The next Frenetic car produced a short lean man, a dark-haired man with a faraway expression and a boyish man who seemed troubled by a secret sorrow. Stephen had to smile at the next arrivals, a couple absurdly and obliviously in love with each other. He noted their transport with surprise—a laundry van.

The athletic boy came out of the pavilion and threw himself catches. Slowly other Frenetics joined him and began a disorganized fielding practice. The man from the chauffeured Mercedes did an imitation radio commentary. It was uncannily accurate. Someone threw an immense skyer. The three nearest Frenetics all called 'Yours!' and the ball fell to earth without interference.

'Your team could be up against it,' said Stephen.

'You're in for a lot of surprises,' said Antony Scorer. ; The two captains tossed up. 'We'll bat,' said Frank Wall.

'We're fielding,' said his opposite number. 'Joe, will you keep wicket?' he asked the man with the secret sorrow. 'Hell, did somebody put the gloves in the kit last week? Pat and John to open the bowling? How many are we?' He tried several futile counts.

'Oh for God's sake, keep still ... One... two...'

His counting problem was solved when a final car screeched into place. A perspiring, overweight man bounded out and held the door open for a beautiful woman, who gave everyone a vague smile.

'Made it darling awfully sorry Joel' he said in one breath, and dived into the car for a basket and a rug.

The woman quickly seized the basket and strode off towards a place in the sun, still smiling vaguely. She stopped and indicated wordlessly that the man could spread the rug.

'We're starting, Alex,' said the captain tightly. The latecomer scurried back for his cricket bag, waved at the woman, who ignored him and lay face down on the rug, and darted into the pavilion. Frank Wall and an ancient came out to umpire. The Frenetic captain (identified to Stephen by Antony as Joel Hegarty) inspected the wicket with Pat Hobby. Pat asked for the pavilion end.

Joel Hegarty organized three slips, gully, mid-wicket, square leg and a deepish leg slip. Without being asked the long-haired man with the scowl took up position at insanely silly mid-off. Joel then realized that he had given himself no place in the scheme of things and wandered in the direction of cover. The gray-haired man who had practised the forward defensive stroke stepped out to take first strike for Upton Cerney.

'Number one is Seb Bulmer, number two is Ted Smith,' called out Sam Gribben, who had abandoned the hot scorebox to Antony.

'Bowler's name is Hobby,' replied Antony. Stephen focused his long lens onto the bowler's wicket. He watched Pat Hobby mark out his run. The change into whites had transformed his personality: no longer a hangdog figure but a hired gun.

His first ball (delivered after ten accelerating paces, a pivot and a follow through which threatened silly mid-off) leapt off the pitch and took the outside edge of Seb Bulmer's bat. It was a straightforward catch to first slip, the passenger in the Mercedes.

He dropped it. Pat Hobby pounded the earth, then looked up to see the offender. 'Bad luck, Arthur!' he called loudly.

Stephen was puzzled. 'I'd have been livid.'

Antony Scorer explained. 'Pat Hobby is an out-of-work screenwriter, trying to sell a pilot script for a new TV series. And Arthur Fraser at slip happens to be the head of Megalopolitan Television.' He coughed. 'What is not generally known is how Arthur rose to that position.'

Lift Off

There were many things which Arthur Fraser used to hate about his job, but the worst of them was the lift.

He worked in a tall building called Excelsior House. Both the building and its lifts were shared between two important enterprises.

Floors 1 to 14 inclusive belonged to Megalopolitan Television. Floors 15 to 24 inclusive belonged to Her Majesty The Queen, who had graciously assigned them to her Department of Internal Revenue and Expenditure (DIRE).

It was never difficult to distinguish the different users of the lifts. Mega-TV employees wore casual clothes but emphatic fragrances. Their men disdained jackets and ties in favour of garish open-neck shirts. They greeted each other in the lift like long-lost brothers and sisters, and complimented each other in exotic language. One especially florid man had a regular set of buzzwords: 'very heavy... very macho... very phallic...'

The DIRE people wore dark clothes. The men had white shirts, ties and jackets at all hours of the day. They smelt of government-issue soap. DIRE people were silent in the lift until safely past the fourteenth floor, when observations about trains or the weather were permissible.

Arthur was a minor official of DIRE. His boss was an incompetent martinet, who had blocked his bids for transfer or promotion. His work was routine, his prospects negligible. Day after day he travelled up in the lift. He studied every word and gesture of the Mega-TV people. The florid man's catchphrase lodged in his brain: 'very heavy... very macho... very phallic.' It became his mantra too, his hope of reincarnation in another life-form.

Arthur would sometimes imagine himself getting out on one of the Mega-TV floors. But he recognized this as an unattainable fantasy. Day after day the lift doors would seal him into his prison beyond the fourteenth floor.

Worst of all were the days when Arthur had to share a lift with the head of Megalopolitan Television. Come shine, come rain, he wore Ray Ban sunglasses, a Patek Phillippe watch and a real (not Hong Kong) Vuitton briefcase—symbols of everything Arthur would never become. His presence in the lift would reduce all other Mega-TV employees to jabbering servility. The florid man would instantly blurt out his senseless catchphrase: 'very heavy... very macho... very phallic.'

Not so Arthur. The sight of the Mega-TV chief would rouse him to helpless fury. He would stare at the man with an intensity of longing and resentment. One day he found himself alone in the lift with the Big Cheese. For all his power and status the man could not meet Arthur's look, but rummaged instead in the expensive briefcase before fleeing to the 14th floor.

There were a few consolations in Arthur's life. One was playing cricket for the Frenetics. He was a fast bowler. By picturing his boss facing him at the batting crease he could psych himself into awesome pace.

The other was Ackford. He was a colleague in DIRE. Although unimaginably senior, Ackford had succeeded year after year in avoiding promotion by pointing out the stupidity or cowardice of his superiors. He was marooned in the same section as Arthur, and treated their foul boss with pitying contempt. Ackford had a gift for rage. Anything at all could trigger it off—a lying politician, the state of the London Underground, a pretentious novel, a malfunctioning photocopier could send him into a fugue of disgust and loathing. But neither cricket nor Ackford could remove Arthur's longing for escape into the glorious lower world.

One day he nearly made a break for it. He was late for work and found himself all alone in the lift. Mechanically he pressed the button for his floor. But mysteriously the lift stopped at the sixth, one of the television floors, even though nobody was waiting.

The doors stayed open a long time. Arthur gazed out into the promised land. Happy people were hurrying and chattering. Somewhere a telephone chimed. Was it for him? The bell seemed to be calling: turn again, Arthur.

He stepped forward. But on the edge of freedom a sickening thought occurred to him. My clothes. Gray suit, drab shirt, neck buttoned up, wretched striped tie. I'd be a marked man. They'd know I was trying to escape. They'd gun me down like a dog…

Suddenly he heard a familiar voice. 'Very heavy… very macho… very phallic,' the florid man was calling over his shoulder as he entered the lift. Arthur shrank back into the shadows.

Arthur described this experience to Ackford in their coffee break. Ackford closed his eyes and said 'I will discuss the problem with the escape committee.'

Several weeks passed. For some reason Arthur's boss took against him even worse than usual. Day after day he hovered like a cassowary over Arthur's desk, opening his eyes to say 'I am displeased.' Then would follow a stream of abuse, never as well constructed as Ackford's rages, but demeaning and ridiculous. He took to setting Arthur trivial errands such as fetching stationery or emptying waste paper baskets. Ackford remarked mysteriously 'I shall have to use my powers as Senior British Officer.'

One day Arthur's coffee break was interrupted by their foul boss. 'Fraser. There's a visitor for me in reception on the ground floor. A Mr Bradshaw. Go and fetch him.'

Ackford, who was following with a tray of coffee, suddenly

tripped over his own feet. Arthur was drenched in coffee. It was too lukewarm to do him personal injury, but his jacket and tie were wrecked and his white shirt acquired a crazy tan stain.

'Frightfully sorry,' said Ackford insincerely. 'Here, give me your jacket and tie.' Arthur obeyed. 'I'd better get Mr Bradshaw,' Ackford continued, but (as he predicted) their boss sputtered 'I said, Fraser.'

Arthur headed for the lift. Several DIRE colleagues eyed him curiously. Instinctively, Arthur covered his neck. The civil servants left on or before the 15th floor and were replaced by television people. They smiled at Arthur, and one called out 'Love the psychedelic shirt.' Another sniffed. 'Interesting fragrance. Almost like coffee.' Arthur beamed. Good old Ackford. He's made me look like one of them...

The lift stopped at several floors. It became choc-a-bloc with television people. At the third floor they all poured out. The doors stayed open. Arthur hovered on the edge. Then he fingered his psychedelic white-and-tan shirt. With one bound our hero was free.

But once on the alien floor Arthur was seized by panic. What do I do now? Where do I go? I don't have an office here...

However, his dilemma was solved when a secretary bustled up to him. 'You're late. BC's already started the meeting.' He followed her into a conference room. The Big Cheese of Megalopolitan TV was in the chair. Some two dozen men and women were in attendance. Arthur slipped into an empty place. No one recognized him as an interloper. There seemed to be no papers for the meeting: the lingering civil servant in Arthur was shocked. He listened to the discussion, and tried to make sense of the proceedings.

Soon he concluded that they were planning a new action-man series around a detective or a secret agent. He heard one man say 'I see this character in non-stop action.

Maybe he gets thrown around, maybe he has a lot of falls, but he always comes back for more.'

Another man chimed in 'Great, but we also have to see him in bed. Every week a big close-up in bed.'

A woman said 'I like the food sequences, Research says that gives major audience-identification, but I wonder if we are going too heavy on the carbohydrates?'

'Not a problem,' a third man disagreed. 'Goes with the character. They have to see him as big, warm, protective, very *physical*.'

There was general agreement, and then the Big Cheese spoke. 'We have a basic character. Now we have to refine him. Let's give him some props. What kind of props do you see for him?'

The question was aimed only at Arthur. He swallowed air and closed his eyes. He re-opened them and caught sight of the florid man. It gave him inspiration. 'Well, we all see our hero as ... very heavy, very macho, very phallic. That's the kind of prop I see for him. I see him all the time toting a big ugly black gun, a big ...Luger... that's it, very heavy, very macho, very phallic...'

There was a long, stricken silence. Finally the Big Cheese said 'Heavy? Macho? *Phallic*? For a *teddy bear*?'

Arthur turned cold. He had betrayed himself. He was the only person in the room not to know that they had been talking about a TV series for young children. He could see them all pointing and murmuring. At any moment he expected to be denounced as an impostor. The Big Cheese silenced the hubbub with a voice of doom.

'I like it.'

'It's a great idea, BC,' said the first man.

'A teddy bear with a Luger. This one has legs, BC,' said the second man.

'Way in front of the competition, BC,' said the woman.

'Don't know how you keep thinking them up, BC,' said everyone except Arthur.

The Big Cheese turned to Arthur. 'Go and do me a treatment.'

By now Arthur had recovered from shock. His brain gears were fully engaged. 'How do you expect me to do a treatment in my office?' he asked indignantly. 'It's not fit for a dead pig.'

As he expected, the Big Cheese was furious. He turned to an underling. 'Why the hell hasn't he got a new office? I ordered a new office for him weeks ago.'

'Absolutely, BC. It'll be ready for him right away.'

Arthur's brain moved into overdrive. 'And another thing. I haven't seen my new contract.'

The Big Cheese was furious again. 'I ordered his new contract ready months ago. Do I have to handle everything myself?'

'Ready for signature today, BC,' said the underling. The Big Cheese swept out.

'Give me that treatment tonight,' he ordered Arthur from the door.

Everyone followed him out except the underling, who whispered nervously to Arthur, 'You don't happen to have kept a copy of your new contract? Ours seems to have gone astray.'

'I think I can lay my hands on one.' The underling left, with grateful thanks. Arthur followed him at a distance. People greeted him effusively everywhere, and Arthur heard murmurs 'Teddy bear… Luger… genius!'

Before long Arthur found an untenanted typewriter. He wrote out a 'new' contract for himself at Megalopolitan Television, as a 'creative consultant'. He hesitated over the salary and finally put down a figure four times larger than his civil service wage. That proved his first mistake. The underling accepted it without demur, and Arthur knew he had underpriced himself.

Arthur also typed out a letter to his boss at DIRE. It read simply 'I resign. You are a pathetic little dweeb with a face like a dead gerbil's arse. By the way, top priority file DI 375/b is in the Ha-Ha wouldn't you like to know?' He went down in the lift to post it. At the ground floor there was a minor commotion.

A man in a gray suit was complaining 'My name is Bradshaw. I had an appointment for eleven,' and reception was telling him that he could not enter the lift without being accompanied.

They really should not allow these people in, thought Arthur.

Besides posting his letter, he bought some new informal shirts and trousers and a discreet gold bracelet. He also spotted a new male fragrance, called Macho. He tried it, and lo! it was good.

Freshly appareled and a-perfumed he returned confidently to Excelsior House. Mr Bradshaw was still on the ground floor.

He travelled up in the lift, one floor at a time, in search of his new office. It was hopeless. He could not find his name on any door. But again his problem was solved for him.

Outside one office was a long queue of very small actors dressed as teddy bears, all brandishing stage Lugers. 'Out! Begone!' he shouted, 'I'm not ready to cast!'

Arthur now had his contract, clothes and an office. It only remained for him to write his treatment for BC. Only what the hell was a 'treatment'? He did not dare confess his ignorance. He paced his office futilely for several hours (which, when observed, reinforced his reputation for genius).

Then he set off again on his travels through the Mega-TV floors. At length he found a room piled high with manuscripts. He picked some up and eventually found the answer to his question. It was a yellowing sheaf labelled 'WAR AND PEACE. A Treatment by Pat Hobby. (From an idea by L Tolstoy).'

Someone had added, in large felt tip letters, the word

NO! but it told Arthur that a 'treatment' was a simple narrative with outline characters and scenes. That evening Arthur was able to hand BC a treatment for a new series called Ted Luger.

By the weekend Arthur blended perfectly into the Megalopolitan landscape. His foul ex-boss failed to recognize him in the lift. Neither did Ackford. On Saturday Arthur caught a plane and sent Ackford a postcard from just inside the Swiss frontier with Germany.

'Ted Luger', written and created by Arthur Fraser, became a worldwide smash. A gun-toting teddy bear in a dirty mac and battered fedora proved a natural for character merchandising. The profits of Megalopolitan rocketed and Arthur got a piece of the action.

In spite of workouts in the Mega-TV gym he began to put on weight. He continued to play for the Frenetics but he was too happy to bowl fast any more. Gradually he settled into the slips and drifted down the batting order. But his appearances were still greatly welcomed. Frenetics noted his new-found generosity at the bar. And for the first time Arthur showed a gift for mimicry. His uncanny imitations of famous cricket commentators often forced Antony Scorer to record 'Laughter Stopped Play'.

Arthur resumed contact with Ackford. His rages were as brilliant and instructive as ever.

The Big Cheese of Megalopolitan continued to call conferences. At one of them he berated the network's sports team.

'We're getting creamed by the BBC every weekend. When are you people going to come up with a fresh idea?'

Arthur suddenly found himself saying 'The BBC always does big matches, and we try to compete. Why don't we do a very small match instead? This weekend the BBC will have the Lords Test Match. Why don't we send a crew to a village match somewhere? We don't make fun of it: we show the highlights with an absolutely straight commentary.'

BC loved the idea, and that weekend Mega-TV showed highlights of the Frenetics match against the village of Little Parvum. Arthur supplied commentary, and the nation was puzzled over how Richie Benaud, Brian Johnston, Fred Trueman and the others had managed to visit Lords and Little Parvum on the same afternoon. The experiment was a huge success. Every weekend to this day a Mega-TV crew finds an amateur team and gives them star treatment (although Arthur has recruited fresh young talent to imitate the commentators).

Arthur's next triumph was the comedy series, Mr Meen. Set in a civil service office (portrayed with astonishing realism) with an incompetent martinet in charge, it proved an excellent vehicle for Rowan Atkinson.

With each success Arthur wrote himself a new contract. The second series of Mr Meen brought him to Number 2 in Megalopolitan, just below the Big Cheese. Arthur's greatest coup was yet to come.

The Big Cheese took another meeting. This time his wrath was directed at the current affairs team. 'You're all pussycats! When did we last do a programme which made people sit up? I'll tell you—Jane Fonda's exercise video!'

Arthur broke in quietly. 'We have a lot of angry viewers. They get angry about all kinds of things, from Mrs Thatcher to a blocked drain. But we have no one who can articulate their rage for them. Everyone on Mega-TV is so bland.'

'And of course you know someone who isn't bland?' sneered the head of current affairs.

'As it happens, I do.' And that is how Ackford became a television personality, adopted as the nation's catharsis. Mr Angry... The Volcano... the Rambo of Rage...

At Arthur's insistence Ackford was given an hour a week straight to camera, free to let rip on anything or anyone who had enraged him. He quickly made Robin Day and Brian Walden seem like electronic blancmange. His first interviews reduced two Cabinet ministers, a bishop and the head of London Underground to sobs of contrition. He regularly threw people off the air for lying.

'You may not be able to help telling lies,' he told one foreign head of state, 'but try not to tell stupid ones!'

Arthur by now had been credited with Megalopolitan's most popular programmes. It was time for his final move. At a meeting with the company's directors he let slip that he had received an offer from Granada. The next day the trade papers announced his appointment as head of Megalopolitan, in succession to the Big Cheese, who was asked to write a history of the company.

Arthur became the new monarch of the lifts. He adopted Ray Ban sunglasses, a Patek Phillippe watch and a real Vuitton briefcase. His presence reduced all Mega-TV employees to jabbering servility. The florid man continued to chant his mantra 'very heavy... very macho... very phallic.'

Only one thing blighted Arthur's life. From time to time he had to share the lift with a young civil servant from DIRE. This man would stare at him with an intensity of longing and resentment. For all his new power and status Arthur could not meet the young man's look, but rummaged instead in the expensive briefcase, before fleeing to the 14th floor. In his vast office, surrounded by awards for his programmes, Arthur would sometimes break into a cold sweat.

One day this young man will travel in the lift in an open-neck shirt and no jacket. He will step out on the third floor, into a script conference, and produce a brilliant idea. He will talk his way into an office and a contract and in a year's time he will have my job...

It was fated. But then Arthur Fraser had his best idea

ever. He called in his secretary and dictated an urgent memo to the manager of Excelsior House.

'With effect from tomorrow I want the civil servants in the building to use a separate lift.'

'And that's it,' said Antony Scorer. 'Arthur Fraser is head of Megalopolitan to this day. Oh, and one other thing. That fellow Bradshaw is still waiting for somebody to take him up in the lift.'

Pat Hobby Runs Out Of Luck

The rest of Pat Hobby's opening over was equally cruel. Seb Bulmer groped and missed repeatedly, but his stumps stayed intact. In his second over the ancient umpire refused an lbw appeal off a yorker. He then conceded two fours off an edge over the slips and a Chinese cut.

The other opening bowler—John Morrow—was the father of the twelve-year-old boy. He was given only two slips but the insanely silly mid-off took up position for him, again without being asked. After a short lumbering run, followed by a grunt, John bowled at just above medium pace, very accurately. Stephen was amused by the grunt, but his camera had eyes only for Pat Hobby.

'Even I can tell he's a magnificent bowler.'

'We're lucky to have him,' said Antony Scorer. 'A few seasons ago Pat swore he would never play again, after the match which ruined his life…'

It had always seemed unjust to Pat Hobby that his only lasting gift was for playing cricket. In fifteen years he had lost twenty-three writing jobs, four houses, two wives and many weekends, but he had never lost his outswinger. Pat Hobby could no longer create stories, or scenes, or characters, or dialogue. But the hands that froze over a typewriter could still put the devil into a cricket ball, to the great benefit of the Frenetic Cricket Club.

In the bar after matches he would accept congratulations with becoming modesty. But sometimes he could also be heard to murmur 'Sure, but what's in it for me?'

High Summer once again found Pat Hobby 'between jobs'. His hopes now rested exclusively on his screenplay. Pat looked at it four or five times a day. He had sunk almost all his remaining capital into having it properly typed, reproduced and bound. The screenplay was, at least typographically, a beautiful piece of work. Pat loved to finger the orange binding, with the little window cut out to reveal the title, KILLER WITH STYLE, and then, four lines down, A Screenplay by Pat Hobby. And so indeed it was—although another writer had contributed heavily to the plot, the characters and the dialogue. A Screenplay by Pat Hobby. All he had to do was to sell it.

Ten years earlier in his career he could have made any one of twenty—no, thirty—phone calls, 'Hi, it's Pat Hobby, I'd like to pitch you a screenplay', and been seated forthwith in twenty—no, thirty— executive offices.

But now his telephone calls had a habit of getting lost in clacking switchboards. When he called in person his journeys ended in reception. When he sent letters to friends and ex-associates in film or television strange underlings would send terse replies, underlings who know not Hobby, or knew him too well.

Pat Hobby had no agent. His last one, who had taken him on for sentimental rather than gainful motives, had confessed himself 'unable to fully get behind' Pat's work.

Since then Pat Hobby had acted for himself. He told friends outside of film and television that he preferred to be without an agent: 'in my business you do better with the personal touch.' But it was hard to apply the personal touch if you never got to see anybody.

It being High Summer Pat Hobby found himself not only Senior Professional but also acting Captain of the Frenetic Cricket Club, since all other officials were on holiday.

On that forthcoming Saturday he would be leading the Frenetics against the village of Great Sanborn. Great Sanborn was (and remains) a village of considerable beauty, where Oxfordshire decides to pack it in and leave the rest to Warwicks or Northants. At long long on (or deep deep third man) there is a shimmering lake. At extra extra cover (or deep deep mid wicket) is the handsome and licensed pavilion.

It was a popular fixture. Seventeen players besides Pat Hobby had volunteered to play in that year's match. In making his final selection Pat Hobby eliminated seven to whom he owed money.

Pat Hobby was a great believer in practice. He never missed a session with the Frenetics and often turned out alone at the cricket nets, ready to bowl at anyone who wanted it. He had a very useful gift of being able to bowl, at will, just below the ability of any opposing batsman.

He used this gift in a mixture of charity and self-interest. He genuinely liked to see people enjoying themselves. But he had also found that strange batsmen would often stand him drinks if they had previously thrashed his bowling in the nets. One man, a television producer, had even given him a job.

On the Wednesday before the Great Sanborn match Pat Hobby was back at the nets, alone. He had spent a futile morning in MGM's London building, clutching his Screenplay in reception.

Finally he had given up and taken the Screenplay home. He had exchanged it for his cricket bag, and put on sporting clothes topped by a T-shirt suggesting his connexion with a recent blockbuster motion picture, and walked (saving bus fares) to the nets.

Despite the beautiful day only one net was occupied. A batsman was waiting for someone to bowl to him. With annoyance Pat Hobby observed that he was about eleven years old. Pat was fond enough of children but none of them had ever stood him a round of drinks, still less offered him a job.

'Hello,' said Pat Hobby briefly, and sat down.

'Hello,' said the boy equally briefly, and rehearsed a few dashing cover drives against an invisible bowler. Pat Hobby looked at him. The boy was fair-haired and well-fed. Then Pat took in some more interesting details: the boy's trainers, bat, pads, and gloves, all very expensive and, despite the lateness of the season, brand-new.

Pat rapidly costed the equipment and said 'Do you need someone to bowl at you?'

'I don't know where my daddy is.'

At the bank, thought Pat Hobby, but all he said was 'Here,' and picked up an old cricket ball from his stuff. He walked to the bowler's end of the net. 'Do you want a guard?'

'Middle and leg.'

Pat gave it to him.

'Not fast,' the boy added as Pat tramped back to his mark. Pat stopped after four paces, ambled up to the wicket and, remembering the boy's rehearsal of cover drives, served up a half volley on the off stump. The boy stepped back towards square leg and the ball removed an unguarded off stump.

Pat Hobby spun round to salute the imaginary hysterical crowd at the Pavilion End. He started his radio commentary: 'A disaster for England! Garner strikes with his first ball, clean bowled, England nought for one...' But he trailed off when he saw himself watched by a tall, fair-haired man of about forty.

'Daddy!' said the boy. And Pat Hobby said, in a very small, faraway voice, 'George Galvan.'

George Galvan... A montage of credits and achievements shimmered before Pat Hobby's eyes. 'Produced by George Galvan': fifteen feature films, two of them Oscar-decked ... 'Mr George Galvan, the new Chairman of the British Film Development Board, making a point to the Prime Minister' ... 'Mr George Galvan whose company announced plans to make a dozen original British films'...

George Galvan. Master of the Destiny of A Screenplay by Pat Hobby, who has just clean bowled his son, first ball.

'You weren't ready for that, were you?' Pat gabbled to the boy. 'It came out of the trees, it took a weird bounce, the surface of these nets is terrible, there's an awful glare... Look, try another one.'

But the boy made no move to return the ball.

'Go on, Carlo,' said George ingratiatingly. 'I'm sure he won't bowl fast.'

Too right, brother, thought Pat Hobby. He held out his hand and with a winning but lopsided smile to conceal a badly-filled tooth said 'Isn't it George Galvan? Pat Hobby. The writer. We met at the Academy dinner when you got the award for Destiny Rides Again. Pat Hobby.' George Galvan repeated 'Pat Hobby' slowly and gazed at Pat's T-shirt.

His eyes opened wider. 'Did you work on ET?'

Pat looked blank for a second and then gazed himself at his T-shirt. He said, truthfully but economically, 'It's not easy working with Spielberg. This T-shirt is all I got out of ET.' He looked back at the boy.

'Ready for another?'

'My son, Carlo,' said George Galvan proudly. 'Charles really but he decided on Carlo. He loves cricket. I'd like to get him some coaching.'

A script began to form in Pat Hobby's head. A few sessions at the nets... Carlo showing off his new strokes to a grateful father... an invitation for Pat to chez Galvan... Pat pitching The Screenplay at George Galvan over brandy and cigars.

He picked up his cricket ball. As he walked back to his mark George Galvan said 'You've no idea how clever he is. I've got stacks of readers but nobody can judge a script like Carlo. I always take his advice.'

Pat Hobby gulped and instantly revised his last scene. He would, instead, pitch The Screenplay at Carlo Galvan, over Coke and chips. Suddenly he remembered another father—a fellow Frenetic—coaching his son at these very same nets. He picked up an empty drink can and placed it one pace behind Carlo's feet at the batting crease.

'This is a *landmine*. If you step back on it you'll be blown up and they'll scrape you off the concrete like a piece of strawberry jam!' Pat Hobby snarled and then smiled secretly at George Galvan. 'You're batting for England. You hit the ball, I give you what the shot is worth. I'm umpire, I give you out, you're out. Remember the landmine. You can step forward, or back and across, but never backwards. You have middle and leg. Play!'

Carlo was lbw third ball but umpire Pat Hobby was unsighted by a gnat. Carlo was 'missed' by the imaginary slips and cover point. Carlo was hit in the tummy and had to be revived by a drink. But Carlo also scored runs. Pat Hobby credited him with many fours because of the 'fast outfield'. He resumed commentary on Test Match Special. 'Garner to Galvan, who's on 96. Garner bowls his fast yorker, but Galvan steps out, drives, straight past the bowler, four runs, that's his hundred in his first test for England, the crowd go mad…'

Then Pat shook hands with the boy and said, in his normal voice. 'Well batted. You didn't step on the landmine. Lovely straight drive for your hundred.'

'Would that really be a hundred?'

'Definitely.'

They all sat down.

'Do you play for your school?' Pat Hobby could see the start of tears as the boy replied 'They said Spotty Evans was better than me.'

'Spotty Evans must be a good player.'

'I wish I could play on a team.'

Then Pat Hobby did a wicked thing.

'My team is two players short this Saturday. Would you both like to play?' and he told the Galvans about the

Frenetics and the Great Sanborn match and how much the team needed a punishing middle-order batsman who could score centuries.

After a brief round of pleading by Carlo, George Galvan accepted for both of them, cancelling a prior engagement with a theatrical knight. There was one problem. All of the Galvan cars were either coughing in their stables or otherwise engaged on Saturday: could they both have a lift to Great Sanborn?

'I can pick you up in my car,' said Pat Hobby. Arrangements were made, telephone numbers exchanged.

Before they all departed, George Galvan murmured to Pat 'You've made his day. I won't forget it.'

Pat Hobby forced himself not to mention The Screenplay there and then. Saturday would be better. The boy chattering on the drive home about his big match (must fix it with Great Sanborn for him to get a few runs, thought Pat Hobby), and then Pat would absent-mindedly mention The Screenplay and pull a copy out in the car and the three of them would kick it around in a companionable sort of way and then George Galvan would offer to produce it...

There were only two obstacles. Pat was surplus two Frenetics and minus one car. His car, a relic of his days of regular jobs, had gone into the garage with a deficient alternator. There was now nothing wrong with the alternator but there had been a slight fault in Pat's cheque. He needed to get his car back. As to the two surplus Frenetics, Pat hoped that the problem might cure itself. It was common for members of the team to beg off at short notice with attacks of flu or anomie or visiting relatives. Pat phoned each of his selections in turn.

'Sure you're OK? No fever or delirium?' he asked hopefully. But, curse it, everyone was eager to play at Great Sanborn. Finally he asked the two most amiable members of the side to de-select themselves in exchange for dinner for four. Another hole in Pat's bank balance... but worth it.

He was certain that George Galvan would pay generously for the option on The Screenplay. To solve his car problem Pat went to the only person who might lend him £125.

His more recent ex-wife pushed aside his flowers and asked simply 'How much is it this time?'

'Listen, I'm playing cricket, I'm bowling at this kid and his dad turns up and guess who he turns out to be, guess?'

'Pat. I don't have to read your screenplays any more. No story, no setting, no characters. Just the money. How much?'

'Two hundred and fifty pounds.' (Pat was wise enough in the ways of film finance to double the budget). 'It's an investment, look, all I need is my car back and I am certain, straight-up, certain to sell my screenplay to George Galvan.'

'Pat. I am not giving you £250. You need a car, you can borrow mine. Be careful, Pat. I love that little car. If that little car does not stay in one piece, you won't either.'

'Is that *your* car?' asked Carlo Galvan in amazement when Pat turned up on Saturday morning.

An apricot Renault 5 with handpainted flowers was indeed an unlikely vehicle for a fast bowler. Pat had managed to remove various stickers in favour of liberating women but he could do nothing about the flowers.

'Take a look inside,' he growled. He had prepared the interior with some care. His ex-wife's magazines had been replaced by three copies of Wisden Cricketers Almanac, for the three years that he had been in the Reppingham School First XI. In his third year P. O'D Hobby had also played for The Rest versus Southern Schools at Lord's. There was also a newspaper photograph of a teenage Pat receiving an award from Gary Sobers and a much-autographed scorecard from a celebrity cricket match, describing Pat as a 'Top TV writer and lethal quickie'.

Finally Pat had included some recent Frenetic scorebooks, with his bowling analyses in Antony Scorer's beautiful hand. Buried in his kitbag, to be produced after the match, was a copy of The Screenplay.

Nervously Pat hummed Among My Souvenirs as both Galvans climbed in. The journey to Great Sanborn passed pleasantly enough. Pat talked about his cricket performances. He was modest, and compared fast bowling unfavourably to other activities, including the writing of screenplays. He stopped for petrol and bought a large consignment of Cokes and Mars bars.

'Big hitters need energy,' he told Carlo. The boy was over-hasty in opening a Coke tin. The drink fizzed out and spoilt the photograph of Pat and Gary Sobers.

'Don't worry at all,' said Pat.

Later the boy began and abandoned a Mars bar. It melted into Pat's ex-wife's cherished upholstery.

'No problem,' said Pat.

As they neared Great Sanborn, Carlo said 'Will I get a bat?'

'Oh yes. Definitely. I guarantee it.'

'I don't just want to field.'

'Of course not.' Pat thought about his Screenplay and weighed his responsibilities. He was Captain of the Frenetics. In principle he should focus on one thing, the defeat of Great Sanborn. In reality, Captain Hobby had one tactical plan: to ensure that both Galvans had a wonderful day. His brain seethed. Where should they bat? Where should they field? Would there be enough tea? Would the sun shine? Would either Galvan get stung by a wasp? How could he make sure the boy got a bat and made some runs?

Wrestling with these problems Pat scraped a stationary milk van. He knocked out one of his ex-wife's sidelights and scratched her paintwork. The Galvans looked up in surprise. 'Damn dog,' murmured Pat Hobby.

At length they arrived at the Duck in Great Sanborn. Pat Hobby tried a joke about the name of the pub. It failed. The other Frenetics were already there. Pat introduced the

Galvans and hurried away to buy drinks. On his return he babbled of green fields and upset a dish of peanuts. His team were worried: they had never seen Pat a victim of pre-match nerves.

'Do you like this pub, George? Is your Coke all right, Carlo? Would you like some sandwiches? I don't know what sandwiches they have? Shall I find out? What sandwiches would Carlo like, George? What sandwiches would he like if they don't have them, George?' said Pat Hobby.

At the pitch his flurry continued. 'Here's the pitch, George. Do you like the lake, George? How about a swim, Carlo? Sometimes they hit balls into the lake and they need a good swimmer to fish them out. Do you like the trees, George? Would Carlo like to climb a tree?'

Pat even found himself saying 'Do you like this village, George, or would you like to play somewhere else?' but neither Galvan appeared to notice.

They changed ('This dressing room all right for you, George?') The Galvans slipped away for a little practice and Pat Hobby gave the other Frenetics a team talk.

'Those two are to have a great match. Especially the boy. Nothing else matters. Okay?' The others stared at him. 'You're my *friends*?'

The two captains tossed. Pat was unsuccessful. Great Sanborn decided to bat. Pat Hobby took care with his field settings. 'Where would you like to field, George? Where would Carlo like to field, George? Close… or … not so close? Oh, don't field there, George, the sun's in your eyes.'

Finally he stationed both Galvans in a glare-free zone, waved vaguely at the supporting cast, and marked out his run-up.

On a hot afternoon, in excellent batting conditions, P O'D Hobby bowled 20 overs unchanged, with seven maidens, taking eight wickets for 56 runs. He scarcely noticed. After every delivery he watched the Galvans. If the ball went past them he shouted 'Good try!' and if it went to them he called 'Well fielded!'

At the end of the innings Pat rushed to his car to extract The Screenplay. He came back with it to the pavilion and was surprised to find everyone applauding him.

'Trust Pat to rush for the scorebook when he's taken eight wickets,' said a Frenetic. Pat grinned and pretended to write something into The Screenplay. He sat himself between the Galvans at tea time. He pushed the cake plate at Carlo. George's cup occupied his attention. 'Are you sure you don't take lemon in your tea, George? They must have a lemon somewhere in the village.'

Pat Hobby rummaged in The Screenplay.

'Can I see the scorebook?' said Carlo.

'What? Oh, ha-ha,' said Pat. 'This isn't the scorebook. No, this would not interest you at all.'

'Can I see?' said Carlo. 'Gosh! "Killer With Style. A Screenplay By Pat Hobby." Look at this, Daddy.' But at this promising point in Pat's affairs the Great Sanborn captain approached him and suggested the start of the Frenetic innings.

In spite of Pat's bowling the Frenetics had to make 164 to win, a stiff task, especially since Pat's selection policy had caused him to discard the three best Frenetic batsmen. He chose a batting order with the same care as his field settings.

'Where am I batting?' asked Carlo.

Pat took a deep breath. 'Number 7.'

There were a few coughs from the regulars and the wicket-keeper tied his bootlaces in a marked manner. Number 7 (as is usual) was the most popular berth in the side, since it almost guaranteed its occupant an innings when the opposing fast bowlers were being rested. Pat Hobby ignored the unspoken comments. He despatched numbers 10 and 11 to umpire.

He had assigned himself Number 5 and George Number 8. He gave his openers instructions ('Score as many runs as you can without getting out') and went off with George to bowl to Carlo. Immersed in pumping confidence into the boy, Pat did not register the early fall of three Frenetic wickets until colleagues rushed over to him with pads. The score was 21 for 3.

'Captain's innings, Pat,' said some fool as they rushed him out to bat.

Pat Hobby certainly wanted to play a captain's innings. But he decided that it was even more important to be dismissed before Carlo came in. Then he could appoint himself umpire and as such increase the boy's chances of survival and runs.

Pat had never paid much attention to his batting. He could normally stodge and survive. His career-best before the match was 29 not out, scored in two hours.

But that day he found himself humming an old army bugle call: I've got to get out, I've got to get out, I've got to get out before Carlo... His feet began to dance to the rhythm. He crashed his first ball, of high pace, for four with a straight drive off the back foot.

Gordon Greenidge could have learnt something from the stroke. Pat increased his score to 10 off the next ball, with a pull over midwicket from outside the off stump. Viv Richards would have been eclipsed. The Frenetics watched speechless, apart from Carlo, who remarked 'Gosh!'

In four overs, P O'D Hobby had passed his career-best. Ten minutes later he had made his first fifty, its progress delayed only when the ball had to be retrieved from the lake. The youngest Great Sanborn fielder did the honours. He was a slim boy barely older than Carlo, and had distinguished himself by his fast pick-ups and throws. Pat's partner backed him up well. They were especially good at snatching short singles. Pat did all the calling, even when the ball was behind him. On that day he was the darling of the gods and could do nothing wrong.

But Pat himself was seized by terror. The Frenetics had

long passed a hundred. Both batsmen were set. It was very likely that they would win before Carlo got a bat, two wickets down. Pat remembered a little voice saying 'I don't just want to field.' Desperately he tried to get himself out. To a straight good length ball, above medium pace, he played a reverse sweep. To his impotent fury the ball rocketed all along the ground for four past third man. A flighty spinner came on. Pat shut his eyes, charged down the wicket and fell flat on his face.

The ball hit his bat and travelled safely past mid-on. Before he could try anything else, his partner was dismissed. Frenetics 122 for 4. Pat felt better. It suddenly occurred to him that he could tread on his wicket. He rehearsed the footwork for this manoeuvre as his new partner took strike.

Alas for Pat! Off the last ball of the over the new batsman was clean bowled. Frenetics 122 for 5. Pat saw Carlo Galvan slowly walking to the wicket. Pat rushed to each of the umpires (both fellow Frenetics) to whisper some instructions. 'No lbw, no caught behind against the kid, and all leg-byes are runs to him, okay?'

Then he went to meet Carlo. The boy was happy and excited.

'You and me, Carlo, that's great. Got your straight drive working?' Carlo nodded eagerly. 'Good ... good. Remember you got a century three days ago, so don't go stepping on any landmines, ha-ha.' The boy skipped off to the striker's end and asked for 'Middle and leg.'

The umpire gave it, then looked at his hand. He was perplexed to find that it contained six stones. 'Oh. Sorry. Over. Yes, over. Rather,' said the umpire. So Pat Hobby took strike again. He was in a sunny mood. Carlo would get an innings, the umpires were squared, he should score a few runs, quite possibly the winning ones. In these circumstances he would undoubtedly be a strong advocate for any screenplay written by Pat Hobby.

He smiled at Carlo, now at the bowler's end. Pat's feet began to skip again, to a new tune. We're in the money, we're in the money…

The bowler delivered.

'No ball!' Pat was distracted by the umpire's call. He mistimed his shot and the ball trickled off an inside edge just past his leg stump. Still in time to 'We're in the money' Pat Hobby skipped down the wicket. Something seemed to be pulling at him, saying 'No … no!'

Pat arrived at the non-striker's end, and was surprised to see a small boy waving at him from a little way down the pitch.

'AAAK!' said Pat. The ball was in the hands of the slim boy with the fast pick-up and throw. Before Pat could say anything more he had thrown down the stumps at the striker's end and appealed.

'I'm afraid you're out,' said the umpire to Carlo Galvan.

'No… no,' said Pat. 'I'm the one out. Really.'

'Nonsense, Pat. You crossed.'

'It was a no-ball.'

'You can be run out off a no-ball. Very bad luck, Carlo. You never need to run a single off a no-ball. And it was your call, anyway. Make Pat buy you a beer.'

But Pat could see tears beginning to well up. The next man in was George Galvan. As he passed his son he asked 'What happened, darling?'

Pat Hobby and the whole of Great Sanborn heard the terrible reply. '*He* ran me out.'

George Galvan looked at Pat Hobby as if he had been served a British Rail sandwich at the Connaught. Pat groaned and beat the earth. The match resumed. George was a correct batsman, if a little out of touch. He called (or refused) runs as if partnered by a retarded teddy-bear. Every call twisted a red-hot skewer into the heart of Pat Hobby. Leaden with woe, he crashed a square cut into the boundary. In a bottomless chasm of despair and self-loathing he straight-drove a six for his hundred and the winning runs.

As Man-of-the-Match Pat spent little time in celebration. Carlo refused all offers of food or drink. He disdained Pat's gift of the match ball. 'I want to go home, Daddy.'

Pat drove them back. They were completely silent throughout the journey. Pat was not invited into the Galvan home. Only a few days later did he realize that he had left The Screenplay in the pavilion at Great Sanborn. He did not trouble to send for it.

Pat sold his car to the garage which was holding it. The proceeds barely covered his bad cheque for the alternator, repairs and cleaning of his ex-wife's car and a good dinner for the Frenetics discarded to make way for the Galvans.

Neither George nor Carlo played for the Frenetics again. Carlo became quite keen on tennis. Pat Hobby has never pitched anything more at a Galvan to this day, whether a script or a cricket ball. His Screenplay was performed with success (but without payment) at the Great Sanborn Annual Village Concert.

Death Wish

In Pat Hobby's fifth over, Arthur Fraser took a neat low catch. Pat's gratitude was profuse until he saw that the ancient umpire had signalled a no-ball. Frustration then made him over-pitch. Ted Smith drove him several times through the covers and even the circumspect Seb Bulmer managed a prod for four.

At the other end John Morrow toiled away, line and length, around two runs an over. Upton Cerney reached 44 without loss. John attempted a quicker ball. It emerged as a long-hop, his first real rubbish. Seb Bulmer whacked it into the hands of the small lean man at midwicket. Nine Frenetics offered the bowler ironic congratulations, but his son rushed up to give him an excited high-five. Forty-four for one.

The new batsman was the swain with the motorcycle, identified by Sam Gribben as Jess McFarland. He took three off the first ball with an ominously proficient late cut. Ted Smith aimed a cover drive at the next delivery. Searching for the ball on the boundary he was astonished to hear an appeal for a catch from insanely silly mid-off. Forty-seven for two.

'That man must have a death wish,' said Stephen. 'You could certainly say that,' said Antony Scorer. 'But his death wish gave him a new life.'

From Smallgood and Long, Solicitors
and Commissioners for Oaths

Dear Mr Harper,

I must begin by informing you that young Mr Smallgood has recently retired, after 43 years with this firm, and that I have been asked to assume responsibility for his clients.

I understand from earlier correspondence that you discovered our name in the Yellow Pages two years ago and thought it appropriate to a firm of solicitors. You may therefore wish to know that we shall continue to do business as Smallgood and Long, and look forward to receiving your instructions as before. I hope to meet you in the near future.

Turning now to your letter of 23rd last to Mr Smallgood, I am most sorry to learn of the end of your relationship with Miss Cork. I am seized of your intention to revoke the will which you made in her favour. However, I must confirm the advice given you by Mr Smallgood in similar situations with Miss Baker and Miss Antropee.

It is not a good idea to make personal comments in a will: they could be held to be defamatory and would then have to be removed before your will could be read and published.

Your new intention is to leave your entire estate to your sole living relative. I shall need the full name and address of the person known as Cousin Charlie, together with details of the conditions which you wish to attach to his inheritance.

With best wishes,
Yours sincerely,
Portia Repton (Miss)

Dear Mr Harper,

Thank you so much for your letter of 2nd last, with its kind remarks. I am delighted that you think Portia a suitable name for a lawyer, although, as you suggest, it has forced me to endure many hackneyed comments (among which I certainly do not class your own).

I have noted your cousin's name and address. As to the conditions you wish to impose, it would be unusual but not unlawful to forbid your cousin from changing the colour schemes of your residence should he wish to occupy it after your death. However, for reasons already familiar to you, it would be wrong to comment in the will on your cousin's taste, however dreadful.

If you would like to discuss the matter further, I hope you will drop into the office whenever convenient.

With best wishes,
Yours sincerely,
Portia Repton (Miss)

Dear Mr Harper,

Thank you for your letter of 24th last. I note your decision to disinherit your cousin in favour of your alma mater, Balliol College. Once again I shall need to know more about the conditions to be attached to the bequest.

With best wishes,
Yours sincerely,

Portia Repton.

Dear Mr Harper,

I am in receipt of your further instructions about Balliol. I must advise you that the courts would be most unlikely to uphold the proposed condition for the bequest, namely the public ceremony in which the Master and Fellows are to fall on their knees in the main quadrangle and beg for your money in piteous tones. I believe that such a condition would be void for public policy, not to mention scandalum magnatum.

I am slightly more confident about your alternative proposal, to leave your money and property to the <u>first</u> college faculty willing to beg for them in public.

However, the clause would be extremely difficult to draft, and I would need to know how you envisage that your executor(s) would enforce its terms and what sanctions would be applied to a cheating faculty. It would be easier to discuss all this face to face. Would you care to make an appointment? All of us at Smallgood and Long would be glad to see you.

With best wishes,
Yours sincerely,

Portia Repton

Dear Mr Harper,

I have noted your reconciliation with Miss Cork, and enclose a draft will in her favour. Perhaps you would let me know if this is satisfactory.

Yours sincerely,
P Repton
pp Cheryl Jones (dictated and signed in her absence)

Dear Mr Harper,

I seem to have had no reply to my letter of six weeks ago. I trust that the will in favour of Miss Cork was to your satisfaction.

I must apologize for failing to answer the implied inquiry in your most recent letter, but will do so now. Under the rules of intestacy, your entire estate would pass to your cousin Charlie.

With best wishes,
Yours sincerely,
Portia Repton

Dear Mr Harper,

I was so sorry to hear about your estrangement from Miss Cork. You may not be surprised to know that I foresee major difficulties with your latest proposal, to leave your entire estate in trust to your pet snake, Pele, during his lifetime.

There are many precedents for bequests to pets, and there is no legal objection to your proposal.

However, I am advised that the lifespan of a garter snake is most uncertain and that, except to the eye of love, one specimen looks very like another. I therefore see a clear danger of personation. Pele's trustees will be handling a large sum of money on his behalf and will have the use of your residence during his lifetime. They would therefore have a powerful motive for concealing his death or escape and substituting another snake in his place. It would be extremely difficult to detect such a substitution, which, if repeated, might frustrate for many years your ultimate intention to leave your estate to the British Herpetological Society.

I am sorry that I keep having to raise difficulties over your will. Once again, I would be delighted to discuss the problems with you face to face.

With best wishes,
Yours very truly,
Portia Repton

Dear Mr Harper,

I am in receipt of your revised instructions concerning Pele. I do feel it was wise of you to reduce the size of the trust in his favour. You now propose several substantial bequests to a Mr Wayne Dwop, of Terre Haute, Indiana, USA, Mr Trust-in-the-Lord

Gumby, of Albuquerque, New Mexico, USA, and Mr Donald Duck, of Leonia, New Jersey, USA, 'as compensation for their unlucky names.' Once again, I shall need full addresses for these legatees. I shall then be able to devise the new will as you request. However, I must ask if you really wish me to incorporate your proposed comments on your futile existence and your preference for snakes over the human race.

A will once proved becomes a publicly available document. Are you certain that you wish your personal feelings to be read by an ignorant posterity? I shall now take my life—and our firm's guinea—in my hands by asking why you find it necessary to make and re-make your will. From your file you appear to be a man of roughly my age and in vigorous health. I have certainly imagined you that way. Can you be certain (as your latest proposed will declares) that you will never be married and have children? In my experience as a lawyer the future is not invariably gloomy. The only certain thing about it is that it lies in the direction of ahead.

With best wishes, as always,

Portia Repton

Dear Mr Harper,

I am sorry that you took exception to my previous letter. I of course accept that you are as free to dispose of your philosophy as you are your real property, subject to the constraints of law. It would be nice to discuss both with you, face to face. Letters in a file are not only bloodless but cumbersome, and it is always more agreeable to have a client who is a real, as well as a legal, person.

Back to business. Your current intention is to leave the bulk of your estate to the Frenetic Cricket Club, and many personal effects to individual members. An unincorporated association such as the club cannot own land, so that if the bequest is to include your own residence I shall have to ask you again to name trustees.

As you suggest, it will be necessary to identify the personal effects beyond doubt, but I do not think you need quite so much detail as 'my Newbery Vintage Bat with which I scored 43 against the Chelsea Arts Club.' On the other hand, perhaps you have two bats of this type? If so, will your executor be able to identify the one which made the 43? Since you intend so many of these individual bequests, it might be well if I inspected the relevant items in person, when convenient.

With every good wish,

PR.

PS I like watching cricket matches. And snakes.

Dear Alan,

I was very glad to receive your latest letter.

As to the directions for your funeral (long-delayed, I hope) I should say first that it is not strictly necessary to include these in your will, which, as I have mentioned before, will eventually become public property. Turning to points of detail:

1) it will not be necessary to obtain a permit under the Public Order Act 1986 for the New Orleans style marching band which is to accompany your weeping cortege. You wish them to play Duke Ellington's Black, Brown and Beige as a dirge: your estate will have to pay a royalty;
2) it is unusual but not unlawful for the deceased to compose his own eulogy;
3) the words on a donor card 'Help yourself, doc' would cover all and any of your organs.

I look forward very much to the match on Saturday. Since I will be working that morning, could you possibly pick me up at the office?

Yours ever,

Portia

'Do you always field so close to the bat?'

'Yes.'

Portia waited for the wine waiter to finish his work. 'Your scorer thinks you have a death wish.'

'Pfah,' said Alan Harper, scowling at a defunct bread roll.

Portia looked him in the face. 'Apart from being better looking, you are exactly the man I imagined from the letters in your file. The man I wanted to meet.'

'Cynical... melancholy... spitting against the wind of destiny?'

'Out of the ordinary.'

'Wrong!' The other diners in the restaurant stared at them and a man eating profiteroles missed his mouth with his fork.

'I hate that phrase. That's what people said at Balliol,' Alan continued more quietly. 'It's been a curse. Ever since Balliol I've led a dreary, empty life. I've achieved nothing. I've … fallen out with everyone who's ever loved me. I've always made the most boring, uncreative choice in everything I've done. The only interesting thing about me will be my death.' The wine waiter returned and hovered. Alan ordered more mineral water to be rid of him. 'That is why I keep remaking my will. When you tell me that a will becomes public property, I'm glad. It's the only thing of mine that will ever be published. By the way, you have never sent me a bill. Do I get a discount for repeat orders?'

'My bill,' said Portia, 'will be payable in the form of transport to every match you play in, and dinner afterwards. The payments to be discontinued when you want. But if you ever decide not to see me I shall make a terrible mess of your funeral and swindle your snake out of his inheritance.'

So for the rest of that season Portia accompanied Alan to Frenetic matches.

And on the following Monday she would carry out Alan's instructions to cut one or more members out of his will: Pat Hobby for missing a catch, Arthur Fraser for showing an Ingemar Bergman film on Mega-TV, Antony Scorer for recording some of his alleged runs as leg-byes. Once he disinherited the lot of them in favour of a Mr Xavier Xerxes Xuereb, of Malta, whose name had caught his eye in a story in the National Enquirer.

But at the end of the season an event occurred which automatically invalidated all of Alan's previous wills. The Frenetics formed a guard of honour for him and Portia outside the church, with an arch of upraised cricket bats.

'I hate to mention this,' said Portia after the honeymoon (in Corfu, for the cricket) 'but you do need a new will.'

'It's made,' said Alan. 'I did some research and I have used the same words as the shortest will ever proved.'

He handed Portia a signed and witnessed document which read 'Everything to wife.'

High-Low

'New batsman is Ray Senior,' shouted Sam Gribben to his colleague, Antony Scorer.

He was one of the would-be Brazilian footballers, athletic and well-balanced. It did not take the Frenetics (or Stephen) long to realize that two high-class batsmen were at the wicket together. All the close fielders bar Arthur Fraser at slip were withdrawn. Even Alan Harper retreated, glaring, to short extra cover. Pat Hobby's misfortunes continued. Another plausible lbw was rejected and a low edge bounced inches short of first slip.

'Well fielded, Arthur,' he called automatically, but with so little verve that Joel Hegarty knew he was ready to come off. At the other end, Jess McFarland watched half an over of John Morrow and then stepped out to drive the next half, all of good length, to the long-off boundary. After a short consultation with his bowlers and wicketkeeper Joel Hegarty replaced Pat Hobby with himself. The wicketkeeper advanced to the stumps, accompanied, with some reluctance, by Arthur Fraser at slip.

The man with the faraway look drifted towards gully. Alan Harper went to silly, but not crazy, point. A short midwicket and extra cover remained within shouting range. All the rest required semaphore.

'Bowler's name, Hegarty', proclaimed Antony. 'This will be interesting. He can be devastating, but it's never certain which side will be devastated.'

Stephen photographed the Frenetic captain gesturing violently at long off, who had strayed out of position to gain the cooling shade of a tree. After moving him, Joel walked back five paces, turned, shimmied sideways and bounced up to the stumps. Two paces before reaching them his right arm began to whirl. It completed 540 degrees and then delivered the ball with a violent turn of the wrist, like a man opening a stubborn jar of pickled beetroot. The ball doodled through the air like a Cruise missile, and Ray Senior lofted it precisely to the tree which long off had been ordered to abandon.

'Was that four?' Antony called out, before the umpire could think about signalling a six.

The umpire concurred. 'Take plenty of pictures,' Antony told Stephen. 'There will be plenty of action. This is a gamble, putting himself on. The only gamble he's allowed.'

'Explain please, as if I could stop you.'

Antony sharpened his red pencil which he used for Joel's bowling analysis and held it up to the sun.

'I've known Joel for ... six years. I was introduced to him by one of my clients, a woman called Donna Clarke. We had a noisy meal in the Chelsea Arts Club, at which Joel talked non-stop about the Frenetics, but then, out of the blue, he asked me to be his accountant.

'I liked him but he seemed a rather ... erratic sort of chap and promised to be a troublesome client. However, before I could reply Donna took me aside and whispered that Joel had a private company which was turning over £5 million a year. Arthur Fraser had arranged for him to get the European franchise for all Ted Luger merchandise.' Stephen whistled.

'Oh yes, this club tends to stick together.

'So, after mature consideration for two seconds, I accepted Joel's offer. Then he made me another one, instantly: would I play for the Frenetics that weekend? Not score, but play and no jokes about my name. And because of that, I volunteered to score for the Frenetics and I've never regretted it, unlucky!' Joel had completely beaten Jess McFarland with a leaping googly which missed everything and yielded two byes.

'Joel was and still is a very popular captain but I noticed a funny thing early on. If the Frenetics batted first he was never allowed to declare. Someone else always took the decision, if it arose. I noted this but never really thought about it till later.

'Joel was and still is mad about his wife and daughters, who were little then, but I noticed soon after I started scoring for him that they stopped coming to matches for a long period. Then they came back. Again I never really thought about this till later.

'Shortly after the return of Joel's family Donna Clarke phoned me. Did I by any chance play poker? She sounded casual but somehow I sensed that it was important. So I said yes even though I had never played the game in my life. Out! Was that caught or stumped?' Antony called to the umpire.

'"Stumped Barnes … bowled Hegarty"' he told Sam, as Ray Senior trudged back to the pavilion, still rehearsing the six which the ball had deserved. Upton Cerney were 95 for 3.

Frank Wall was the next batsman. Captain bowled to captain. Suspecting hidden demons, Frank patted back four very slow half-volleys.

'Donna Clarke invited me to play poker at Joel's that Thursday evening. There had been a regular school, but the fifth player had been posted to the European Community in Brussels, to fight for British asparagus against all comers, and they needed a replacement. So I accepted. Again Donna hinted that it was terribly important, and said would I be absolutely certain to tell her if I had to drop out.

'So I bought a book about poker and dealt myself a few

hands, and by Thursday I felt I would at least not make a fool of myself.

'On the Thursday I met the other players at Joel's house. Besides Donna and Joel there was Arthur Fraser, a rising executive at Mega-TV, and an elderly Vietnamese gentleman called Mr Nguyen.

'Joel had a very nice house near Ladbroke Grove. His wife Eileen poured us drinks and we all took a quick look at their little girls, who were asleep. Then Eileen excused herself and left us to play.

'Joel had set up everything beautifully. Proper lighting, green baize cloth on the table, new plastic playing cards. And he had taken down the mirror from the wall behind the table. Little touches like that mean a lot in poker.

'All the others bought chips. I hadn't been warned about the stakes, and I was worried to see each man buy at least £100. But I tagged along.

'Joel said "Gentlemen, the game is five-card stud", as if we were all in The Cincinatti Kid, and we got under way.

'I played very cautiously that first game, and watched the others. I noticed early on that Joel could not bear to be out of a hand. Arthur and Donna were very competitive against him and there were a lot of big pots.

'Mr Nguyen was even more careful than me. He was prepared to fold early, hand after hand, but when, he had cards he would bet them to the limit.

'At midnight, when we had been playing for about three hours, we had a break and Eileen wheeled in a trolley with expensive cold snacks. By this stage Joel was losing heavily, mostly to Arthur. Donna and Mr Nguyen were a bit ahead, and I was just about even.

'We played again and Joel started to recover. His pile went up, Arthur's went down. Mr Nguyen won two big pots off Joel and then closed up for the rest of the night. Donna got into a head-to-head with Joel over a very big pot, but folded without seeing Joel's hole card. I won a big pot of my own, off Joel, but right afterwards Joel won big over Arthur. At two o'clock three taxis came to take everyone home. Donna told me that two o'clock was the unvarying time limit. By then Joel had lost about £30, Donna was down maybe £20, I was almost even, Arthur was up about £25, Mr Nguyen up about £35.

'In spite of losing, Joel was happy as a clam. As we said goodbye he replayed all the big hands with us. Arthur and Mr Nguyen got into one taxi. I got into another, but before it set off Donna suddenly stuck her head in and said "You are coming next week, aren't you?" and yet again it seemed important. Well, it had been a nice evening, and Joel was an important new client, so I said yes, and Donna scooted back into the third taxi.

'So I went to the game for two more weeks. And it followed exactly the same pattern. Up until midnight Joel would lose heavily. After the break he would recover substantially, either from Donna or Arthur or both of them. Mr Nguyen would end up in profit, through winning a few big hands and sitting quiet the rest of the night.

'After three weeks I was getting proficient at poker and I began to pick up things in the play of the hands. I realized that some very peculiar things were happening after midnight. No, it's left of the tree…' Antony broke off narrative to supervise recovery of a six hit by Jess McFarland. After some minutes (the more experienced Frenetics span out the search to get a rest) Antony was able to resume.

'I phoned Donna the next day and met her in a pub where we knew nobody. "Look," I told her, "why do you and Arthur always play so badly after midnight? And why always against Joel, never against me or Mr Nguyen? Joel is a rotten player and you let him win. Yesterday he tried a really stupid bluff against you, pretending he had three eights. But you had already seen an eight in Mr Nguyen's hand, and you had seen me bet heavily on my two face cards, seven and nine. Pretty obvious I had the fourth eight as my hole card, so he couldn't have it. But you let him bluff you. Why?"

'Donna sighed heavily. "Arthur and I have not been open with you. You are entitled to be angry, although you have lost nothing and I hope you have enjoyed your evenings. But we should have let you in on the secret.

'"Joel is indeed a rotten player. He does not understand basic probabilities. He is also a compulsive gambler. As you can imagine, this combination is potentially lethal. His cricket team know it, that's why they never let him declare.

'"Joel used to gamble crazily on anything and everything, in casinos, racecourses, betting shops, arcades, anywhere at all. He would make weird bets with strangers on a train. He would lose regularly, big amounts, but he still believed he was a genius. Eileen walked out on him several times and took the girls, and he always swore he would give up, but then he would drop a thousand pounds at the dog track. That was really some achievement, I mean, if you bet on dogs completely at random you would not lose that much money, but Joel had some daft 'system' to help him lose. Anyway he was heading for ruin and Eileen was ready to leave him for good.

'"Arthur and I go back a long way with Joel, Arthur through the Frenetics and me even longer. So we met and worked out a plan. We would organize Joel a poker game every week. We roped in Mr Nguyen and Arthur got David Forrest, the chap who's just gone to Brussels.

'"Arthur and I settled on two rules for the game: lots of excitement and action for Joel, and a guarantee that he would never lose much money. We never told the other two. They were allowed to play for real. David was on a rotten salary and Mr Nguyen was a refugee and they both needed the money. But when Joel's losses got out of hand either Arthur or myself or both of us would contrive to lose money back to him. I'm pretty sure David and Mr Nguyen knew what we were doing but they were on a good thing and kept quiet. Also I think they liked Joel and wanted to keep his family together.

'"We did let Eileen into the secret. We said that the game might just give Joel enough action each week to end his need to gamble anywhere else. So she agreed to give him one more chance.

'"And thank God, the plan actually worked. Joel got a terrific buzz out of the game. It wasn't just the action, it was the rhythm and the ritual, setting up the room, being a serious rambling-gambling man out of New Orleans ... it satisfied him. He actually stopped gambling apart from the game.

'"There you have it. The game is a fraud. But it has saved a man's marriage and possibly his life. Now you owe nothing to Joel, or me, or Arthur. You are free to walk out of the game. Or you can stay and play for real, like Mr Nguyen. You can take Joel to the cleaners. Arthur and I will pick up the bill. We can afford to. But the game must continue. If you drop out we will find a replacement."

'I was amazed. I had had some experience of fraud as an accountant, but I had never known a fraud designed to rob the fraudsters. But I went to the game next week. I was still confused. I played very badly and lost, even to Joel. And then Eileen came in and he replayed the hand I had just lost, and it suddenly became clear to me that I had to stay with the game.

'I played for a few more weeks. No change in the pattern, except that Mr Nguyen hit a streak and became a big winner. Since I was a little ahead too, that meant that Donna and Arthur took a real beating, having to cover Joel's losses as well as their own.

'Even though they were rich I thought it was unfair on them. I felt uncomfortable profiting from their philanthropy. Next week Mr Nguyen was a heavy winner again and I decided that after the midnight break I would make my contribution to reducing Joel's losses. Unfortunately Joel and Eileen were bustling around us and it was impossible for me to tell Donna or Arthur about my decision.

'By midnight that evening Joel was already down £100 and he was going to need a lot of help from Donna and Arthur and me for the rest of the evening. But as luck would have it, right after the break Donna and Arthur both had a long run of terrific hands, so terrific that even Joel realized he was out of it and folded early. He stopped trying to fill his inside straights or pull off his crazy bluffs. That stopped him losing any more but it also stopped him making any recovery.

'With only a few hands to go before the two o'clock close, Joel was still taking a bath. Then at last he got some cards, an ace showing and a pretty transparent second ace in the hole. Donna and Arthur had nothing showing but they started betting against them. Mr Nguyen folded. I felt that it was time for my plan, so I came in hard too, when the next card was dealt. Joel caught a pair of threes to show with his ace, the rest of us had nothing. Donna and Arthur gave me strange looks when I kept betting, but I could not say anything at the table, just hope that they would understand that I had decided to help out. But they stayed to the bitter end, and when Joel showed his two pair, threes on aces, and beat our garbage the pot was enormous.

'Joel made enough to wipe out his evening's losses and come out about £60 ahead. He had never made so much on a pot and he was over the moon and into the asteroid belt.

'The next day I got a furious phone call from Donna. What the hell had I been playing at? So I told her and she shouted "You moron! You've ruined everything! Joel now thinks he's on a roll. He's just booked himself a week in Las Vegas."

'Shortly afterwards I got another call from Donna. "Drop everything on Monday evening. Arthur and I have persuaded Joel to have a special farewell game before he takes off. You will be there. Only the rules have been changed. We are to take Joel to the cleaners. Every damn stupid thing he does, every hand, he is to be punished. We haven't told Mr Nguyen. He can play the percentages, like he always does. But you and Arthur and I are going to play the best poker of our lives."

'When I arrived on Monday night I noticed that Eileen and the children were away. Joel was evasive about this. Donna and Arthur caught my eye and whispered "Plan B" as Joel fussed with the drinks.

'The three of us bought double our usual quantity of chips and Joel was pleased. "More spending money for me in Vegas".

Then he made the ritual incantation. "Gentlemen, the game is stud poker."

'After two hands we could sense that Plan B was going horribly wrong. Joel won the first by filling an inside straight. The second he stayed in with garbage and won with three of a kind. And that's how things stayed. Mother Teresa was dealing the cards for Joel that night. Every time one of us got a hand, Joel would top it, flushes, full houses, four of a kind, anything he needed he got. And he kept humming this silly tune "Viva Las Vegas".

'By midnight he had won something over £300. He wheeled in the trolley with the usual snacks. We all thought about the missing Eileen. He had to be stopped from going to Las Vegas, but would his luck change before the taxis came at two am?

'Sure enough, it did. Joel started out with lousy cards and they failed to improve. Then a terrible thing happened.

'Out of the blue, Joel started playing like Mr Nguyen. He folded when he had a lousy hand. "Damn it!" Arthur hissed to me when Joel left for a pee, "This is a hell of a time for him to get smart."

'The pile of chips in front of Joel stayed almost unchanged for over an hour, while Arthur, Donna and I fought useless battles amongst ourselves. Even Mr Nguyen, who was not in on the plan, could sense our frustration. He changed his normal pattern of play and began to bet heavily. But Joel refused to rise to the new challenge. He bet little or nothing. During the long intervals when he had folded he would check and re-check his airline tickets and Vegas hotel reservation.

'At one thirty Joel was still a heavy winner. When he and Mr Nguyen left the room, Donna said "We have to get him interested in the action again. It's the last hope for Plan B."

'When Joel returned Donna said "How about a little fun before we go home? A hand or two of seven-card high-low?"

'Joel was suspicious. "What do you mean, seven-card high-low?"

'We used to play it in the early days, Joel. You remember. Two cards face down for each player, and one face up. Highest face up card bets, others follow or fold or raise. Three more face up cards, round of betting after each. Finally a card face down. Last round of betting. Anyone left in declares if he is going for the highest hand, choosing five of his seven cards, or the lowest. Then everyone shows and highest and lowest split the pot. But you can go High-Low. Pick five cards to make a high hand, another five cards to make a low hand, and if you win on both you take the whole pot, no split. If only one person declares high or low he collects half the pot without showing, unless someone else has gone High-Low. Ace can be high or low but not both, so you can't make a round-the-corner straight, like queen-king-ace-two-three. Got all that?'

'Joel turned it over and agreed. So did the rest of us. Donna shuffled and offered the cut to Joel. With a fine gesture he refused—the mark of respect to the dealer.

'Donna dealt. The order was Mr Nguyen, me, Arthur, Joel, Donna. Two down then a face up. I remember Donna calling out "Eight to the man... nine to the man... king to the man... ace to my left... dealer gets a two. Ace bets." Joel opened with £20. I could sense another ace in his hole cards. Donna said "Your twenty and up twenty." Mr Nguyen folded. I looked at my cards. Joel already had me beaten on the high, Donna on the low. It would cost me £40 to buy another card and they were as likely to improve as I was. I therefore folded. So there were just three left. Joel and Arthur called.

'Donna dealt the next round. "Pair of kings… eight to the ace… three to the dealer." It was now Arthur's turn to open, with the pair showing. He bet £50. Donna said automatically "Your fifty and up fifty." She was in the catbird seat, the only low facing two high hands. Arthur raised fifty again. Joel went up another fifty. Donna raised fifty. This time Arthur called. Joel raised another fifty. This time Donna called too. All the bets were level and Donna could deal the fifth card.

'"Pair of kings and a seven… pair of eights with the ace… two, three, four to the dealer, possible straight…" We knew she was bullshitting, and that she had the low hand. "Pair of kings still to bet." This time Arthur checked. Joel opened with a hundred, Donna raised a hundred, Arthur called. This cycle was repeated several times until, as before, Donna allowed the round of betting to end by calling instead of raising. She dealt the sixth card, face up.

'"Three kings… two pair, eights on aces… pair of twos for the dealer." The same pattern of betting followed, except that this time Joel opened with five hundred. Once again Donna and Joel kept raising and Arthur hung in grimly. By now, of course, the chips were long finished. Each player was tossing giant IOUs into the pot. Finally Donna allowed the betting to close again and dealt the last card. "Down and dirty."

'It was still Arthur to open. This time he kicked in a thousand. I figured that he had either completed his full house or just possibly drawn a fourth king. Donna naturally raised him. With the low hand, she was guaranteed half the eventual pot.

'Joel raised too. That could have meant anything. He could have been trying to bluff Arthur into thinking he had four eights, forgetting that the fourth eight had already shown up, in Mr Nguyen's hand at the very beginning. But Joel might have had a genuine full house. If so, which one? Aces on eights would lose to Arthur's full house (assuming he had made it) but eights on aces would beat it. Or Joel could even have had four aces, which would have made him unbeatable. But it was very likely that Donna had one of the missing aces in the hole cards of her low hand. She had bet hard very early. An ace in the hole would account for that. So Joel hadn't got four aces, in fact, I didn't figure him for three aces... He was trying to bluff Arthur out... And Arthur wasn't going to be bluffed, he knew he was high, he would take Joel to the cleaners and stop him going to Las Vegas and save his marriage...

'While I was working this out, the raises were still going on. There must have been fifty thousand pounds in IOUs on the table. I heard Joel say "Raise you another thousand." Donna raised automatically. I willed Arthur on.

'"I fold."

'I nearly killed Arthur with my bare hands. What a moron! Arthur's stupid teddy bear could have played better. Joel had bluffed him. Joel had won half an enormous pot. Whether or not Arthur could meet his IOUs, it did not matter. Joel would go to Las Vegas and lose everything he had won that evening and then everything else he had.

'Donna called. I could not understand why she was so calm. Joel started to divide the chips and IOUs. "Just a moment, Joel," said Donna. "We do have to declare, high or low."

'Joel looked at his cards and smiled. "In that case I'll go high."

'"High-Low."

'Joel turned green for a moment. But to his credit he was

perfectly calm as he turned up his hole cards and said "Full house, eights on aces."

'"I've got four twos," said Donna and turned up her hole cards to show them.

'Donna had won the entire pot. She sorted Arthur's IOUs from Joel's and counted the chips. Arthur wrote out a cheque. Joel reached for a chequebook too, but Donna stopped him.

'"I am going to hold these markers, Joel, on one condition. You cancel the trip to Las Vegas and take Eileen and the kids to Majorca instead. You know well that it is dishonourable to gamble when someone is holding your markers. I shall not let you redeem these markers, ever. Gentlemen, the game is finished."

'And that's how it stands. Donna still holds the markers and Joel has never gambled again. He has a good business and a happy marriage.

'Arthur told me that Donna never cashed his cheque. But Donna has always refused to tell me if she stacked the deck for that final round of high-low. All I have ever got her to say was "I knew it had to happen."

'But she did tell me, last year, that she was Joel's first wife.'

An Excellent Moment

At the end opposite himself Joel Hegarty tried a series of Frenetic bowlers. First was the man with the faraway look ('Bowler's name, Wyatt', called out Antony.) He was billed as a swing bowler and he moved the ball a long way, off the bat. He was relieved by the small lean man ('Bowler's name, Shaw'), who kept the score in bounds by bowling wide of the stumps. Wicketkeeper Barnes flung himself left and right to prevent byes. Off a rare straight ball Jess McFarland reached fifty.

Encouraged by Frank Wall's circumspection Joel kept himself on and threw the ball higher and higher. Then, like a child discovering that there is a Santa Claus after all, Frank Wall helped himself to a four and a six in one over. Drinks were served at 128 for 3.

Pat Hobby returned, refreshed. Soon he had to shout 'Well tried, Arthur!' again. Frank Wall had edged his out-swinger: Arthur at slip had grabbed it twice and dropped it thrice. He cursed himself, apologized, and then intoned, in the voice of Brian Johnston, 'That must go down as a chance... and it did.'

It was an old joke, which failed to lift the gloom in the Frenetic ranks. Upton Cerney were 144 for 3 with two well-set batsmen on a beautiful wicket. The Frenetic fielding began to wilt in heat and failure. Only the captain and the twelve-year-old boy were still prepared to scamper and dive. All the others except one went about their work with a mask of stoic resignation.

The exception was the man who had arrived late. He walked in little circles in the outfield, tense and muttering.

From time to time he looked anxiously at the beautiful vague woman who had accompanied him, fast asleep on the rug in the sun.

'What's the matter with him?' asked Stephen. Antony busied himself for some time with his beautiful scorebook. Then he said 'Alex Bramley's story is the only one you won't hear from me. You are a writer, you have powers of observation and empathy. You may be able to sense what Alex is muttering to himself.'

I'm not going to get a bowl today. We're getting stuffed but Joel won't put me on to bowl. And he's right. I used to bowl quite well, but I don't any more because I don't play very much any more and I don't play very much any more because she hates cricket. Nobody knows she hates cricket, because she always comes with me to the match, and smiles, and sleeps on the rug, and it's a big joke with everyone: no matter how exciting the match she can sleep through it.

And nobody knows why she always goes to sleep every match. Hell, they must know, but this is England and everyone's far too polite to notice. She'll wake up soon and call out to me 'Alex... Alex!' in that high, clear voice people can hear all over the ground. She only does it if I'm fielding and then she always has something for me to deal with, like where's her suntan lotion, or do I know where there's a chemist and I have to stop and *deal* with it and Shit! I can't field any more. Tim's chasing the ball for me. Joel has to put a twelve-year-old boy next to me in the field to cover for me...

'Well chased Tim, sorry Joel, sorry everybody...'

Every time I play she fixes some engagement the same day for both of us. By mistake. So then we have a little fencing match. I'll say 'Why don't you go without me?' but that won't suit her at all so she'll say the other people live way over the other side of town and there's no public transport near them and they'd have to take her back, which has the bonus of reminding me that she can't drive so if I take the car anywhere she gets stranded at home Damn! That throw hurt my arm.

'Try to keep them to one, Alex.'

Thanks a lot, skipper, you really know how to encourage someone.

Then I offer not to play but she won't hear of it, only ... please ... next time could I make sure she knows the date, and she cancels with the other people and makes sure I can hear her saying 'I didn't know Alex had a cricket match.'

So she's got what she wants. I'm playing cricket but I've bitched up her day and I'm feeling guilty. And she's right. I ought to feel guilty. I work six days a week and the one day we could do something together she has to watch me do something she doesn't like or understand and which I don't even do very well.

But hell, she knew about the cricket before we got married. It's not exactly a surprise, the cricket season. Comes up every April, on the button.

I told her what cricket meant to me when she came to that first match in Cambridge. I can remember my exact words to her. 'Cricket is like a terrible, cruel god. He makes you toil horribly for nothing, he gives you pain and humiliation, and still demands total worship. But sometimes without warning the god smiles on you, gives you the reward you crave. He gives you... an Excellent Moment, a moment when you know you did something absolutely right. Maybe it's a great catch, or hitting one perfect cover drive, it's just... an Excellent Moment, a glimpse of a perfect life,' and that was an Excellent Moment in itself, because I had made a beautiful woman laugh. Shit! not another misfield. No, don't chase it for me, Tim, I'm not a complete fossil yet.

They ran three on my throw. What's the reverse of an Excellent Moment? Everybody's looking at me. Everybody except her. She's fast asleep. If I did have an Excellent

Moment she'd manage to wake up in the middle of it and call 'Alex... Alex!' just to louse it up.

I can see the big Coke bottle beside her on the rug. Looks perfectly normal but everyone must know it's Coke-coloured rum, almost neat. I remember when Tim wanted a swig and she snatched it away from him. Of course they all know.

Because she wants them to know.

I've been a fool. She wants people to see. She doesn't actually take all that much from the bottle. Just enough for people to see: this is what my husband has done to me...

'Tim's ball!' It was mine, really, but thanks, kid. I was miles away.

I understand completely why she hates me. I took her destiny away.

She was the best actress of our generation at Cambridge. 'I am Duchess of Malfi, still...' She stopped the whole theatre dead.

Cal was her lover. Cal was Ferdinand. I was just the front-of-house man. She had a fight with Cal and she married me just to score off him, and I knew it in my heart, but it was still an Excellent Moment for me in the registry office.

I wanted her to go on acting. But she still wanted to score off Cal, so she walked away from his world and pretended that it was fun keeping house for me. But it wasn't. Then she wanted a baby, but we... I couldn't make it happen. So then she did try to get back to acting. But by then all her magic had gone. The Duchess of Malfi couldn't get into daytime soap. Not even commercials. Cooped up with me she'd forgotten how to act.

Being an unhappy wife is now the only role she can play. That's why she stays with me. Me and the team and the other wives are the last audience she'll ever get.

She does not drink to forget, but to remember. To remember what it's like to act. The bottle is a prop, goes with the role.

I suppose I might have caught that. Instead they got another two on my throw.

She is Duchess of Malfi, still, to me. I love her desperately, achingly, just as when I made her laugh at our first cricket match.

There are no Excellent Moments left for either of us. We're trapped to each other. She'll play her starring role as the unhappy wife for ever, with special matinees on match days. Oh God, she's waking up. I'm going to hear her calling out any second 'Alex... Alex!' in that high, clear, *actress*, voice they'll hear all over the ground.

'Alex... Alex! Where's the Kleenex? Alex... Alex! Can you do something about the flies? Alex... Alex! Can you do something about my life?'

'Alex! Alex!' Oh God, everyone heard. That high voice. All right, dear, I'll deal with it. Wait. That's not her voice. That's... Tim. What does he want? The ball's coming to me? Well, get away from me, you bastard, leave me alone...

'Owzaaat!' Out. Run out by five yards. Direct hit on the stumps. We needed to get rid of him really badly, he must have made at least sixty. Thanks, Tim. Thank you, Joel, but you needn't sound so surprised.

'Thanks everyone. I thought it was a good throw too.'

I'll do a deal with her. She lets me play cricket but I cut down my work. I'll take her to the theatre every week and I'll be really catty about any actress of her age. 'My dear, that accent... that lisp... those legs...'

And she'll start thinking she could do better than her, and she'll go to auditions again, and she'll land a part in something, and she'll get a proper audience to perform to, and she won't need to play the drinker and we'll have a real marriage...

'Alex... Alex! What's all the noise about?'

'Nothing really, dear. I did a rather good run-out, that's all.'

Tail Piece

Even after the run-out of Jess McFarland the Frenetics were still gloomy. But in the next over Arthur Fraser accepted a difficult low slip catch from Frank Wall off Joel Hegarty, to the genuine admiration of Pat Hobby. Upton Cerney 152 for 5, and the two best batsmen in full cry had been dismissed by the two worst fieldsmen. The Frenetics felt stirrings of hope. They all stiffened sinews and a few even summoned up the blood.

Matters improved still further when Joel discovered a Spot, the leg-break bowler's Holy Grail. Both of the new batsmen were startled by extravagant bounce. Nat McFarland (brother of the illustrious Jess) soon edged to Arthur Fraser, this time a dolly catch. Pat Hobby was fulsome. 157 for 6.

Number eight for the village was called Reg Custer. It had produced countless jokes about Custer's Last Stand. In retaliation he had adopted long ago a policy of occupying the crease regardless of the state of the game. He had an extra thick pair of pads and thrust one or both violently forward to every ball. Since Joel was now getting a lot of turn the ancient umpire decided, reasonably, to reject every lbw appeal.

Number seven (one Robert Jackson) was another of the footballers, and very strong. When a leg bye brought him to Joel's end he smashed two cross-bat sixes over mid-wicket. Pat Hobby came back into the picture. His first ball hit the Spot and rocketed over the wicketkeeper for four byes. Jackson then took a very short single, to the disgust of

Custer, who was left with four balls from Pat at full steam. Although none of them hit the Spot, three hit Custer.

Young Roy, down at number eleven, looked nervously at the time. Twenty minutes to tea. Perhaps he would not be needed to bat.

But next over John Morrow replaced Joel and bowled the dangerous Jackson with a well-disguised slow yorker. Some people might have thought it a slow full toss but Tim explained clearly to everyone that it was his father's well-disguised slow yorker. 175 for 7. The new batsman was the red-faced wicketkeeper. He snicked a two to third man and was caught behind off a much faster lifting ball. Tim looked at his father in amazement. 177 for 8. Young Roy, already padded up, rummaged feverishly in the Upton Cerney kit-bag.

The next over from Pat Hobby did nothing to ease his nerves. Four balls exploded off the Spot. Custer lurched forward and pulled his bat away. The fifth he tried to hit to extra cover and scored two at fine leg. For the last ball of the over Pat and Joel moved everyone to save a single. Pat concentrated hard and rammed in a yorker. Custer just kept it out: no run.

The reason for these tactics soon became clear to Stephen. The new batsman, Bob Turner, had earned promotion to number ten only because he was forty years older than Young Roy at number eleven. As befitted his name, he was a very fine slow bowler. As a batsman he had earned a career average of 1.35 only because of a polite convention to credit him with a few leg-byes in the last match of every Upton Cerney season.

John Morrow's field was rearranged. Three slips, two gullies, leg slip, backward short leg, short mid wicket (for Turner's frequent miscued pull). Alan Harper went back to handshaking distance from the bat on the off side. Tim Morrow was at short extra cover.

Bob Turner took middle and leg with a regal air. John, to

his disgust, bowled a ball wide of the off stump. The batsman shouldered his bat with a flourish. The second was straight. Bob Turner skipped backwards but left his bat in place. Stephen's camera captured his final pose, like a man clinging to a stuck punt pole, but the ball hit the bat and the stumps were saved. A matching shot edged the third just short of the wicketkeeper. John Morrow made a bad choice for the fourth, a perfect outswinger. Bob Turner got his bat nowhere near it. The fifth was a break-back, and with faultless judgment the batsman let it go, a millimetre over middle stump.

John's last ball was a fraction over-pitched. It awoke some ancestral memory in Bob Turner. He played a magnificent cover drive, but just a fraction too early.

The ball looped crazily into the off side field. Tim took its bearings and started in pursuit. Alan Harper looked up too, marked the ball's flight over his shoulder and realised he could catch it. Turning on his heel, he charged after it, head in air, not seeing Tim. John Morrow took in the situation. He tried to call out but his throat was dry with fear.

Joel's voice screeched 'Tim!' Alan juddered to a halt and Tim caught it at the second attempt.

John rushed over and hugged him tight. It was not until much later that he realized he had taken five wickets in an innings, for the first time since Tim was born. Meanwhile there was some confusion at the non-striker's end. Both batsmen were standing there.

Excited by his contact with the ball, Bob Turner had charged down the wicket for a run without informing his partner. After a conference between the two umpires it was ruled that the batsmen had crossed before Tim had caught the ball. In consequence, with the score on 179 for 9, number eleven, Roy Gribben, had to face a complete over from Paceman Pat Hobby, bowling at the Spot.

'Put down out first ball,' sniggered his brother Sam, from a safe distance. 'He's wetting himself.'

Young Roy had strapped a man's thigh pad to the outside of his trousers and in spite of the hot day he was wearing two thick sweaters. Even after these preparations he looked openly scared. He forgot to ask for a guard, and the umpire gave him centre, in default. The entire field closed in as Pat Hobby began his long, menacing walk back to his bowling mark.

John Morrow stopped play. 'There is a helmet he can wear. Off you go, Tim.'

Tim scampered to the pavilion and returned with a very new boy's helmet, with a visor. John adjusted the straps to fit Young Roy and tapped it lightly to demonstrate its resistance.

Joel pulled the field even closer and said 'You can let it go now, Pat.' Pat Hobby took several steps further back from his mark, and pawed the earth. He bounded up to the wicket, leapt into his delivery stride and (as previously agreed with Joel) bowled a very slow full toss. Surprised at his reprieve from death, Young Roy took a reflex swing at the ball. He top-edged.

The ball hung in the air and started to fall straight towards the stumps. Everyone watched, transfixed. Young Roy was the first to recover his senses. Remembering his helmet, he leaned forward and headed the ball safely away into the ground.

Stephen laughed too much to take a picture, but Antony was furious.

'That could have been caught. I've been waiting all my life to make an entry for Obstructing The Field but the fools did not appeal.'

Plan A having failed, Pat Hobby reverted to more conventional methods. He bowled a very fast inswinging yorker. Young Roy skipped towards the off side and jabbed his bat behind him. The result was a leg glance of startling beauty, and a four. The next ball reared from the Spot.

Young Roy turned pale under the helmet, but kept his eye on the ball as he jerked away.

The next ball he edged, all along the ground, through the slips for a second four. Pat tried another yorker, dug out, correctly, to applause from everyone except his younger brother. Pat's last ball was over-pitched on leg stump. Young Roy pushed out and watched the ball travel towards an empty mid wicket.

'Look for two!' shouted Custer, since the batsman had forgotten to call. A fielder was still in pursuit as they turned after the first run.

'Yes!' bawled Custer. 'This end!' screamed both ends as the fielder gathered the ball. Against all logic he selected the bowler's end, but for the second time that day Alex Bramley achieved a run out with a direct hit on the stumps.

Upton Cerney were all out for 188. John Morrow had taken 5 for 37, Joel Hegarty 3 for 42 and there were two run outs. Pat Hobby, easily the best bowler, had taken no wicket for 55 but he was not distressed.

In his capacity as an unemployed screenwriter he was too busy encouraging the head of Megalopolitan Television to talk through his two catches at slip.

The Undisputed Champion of the World

The Frenetics went into tea with some optimism. Antony Scorer informed them that they had dismissed the last seven batsmen for 36 runs (a record for the Upton Cerney fixture) and that their victory target, 189, was less than they had achieved in four earlier victories that season. Alan Harper pointed out that none of these triumphs had been gained on a pitch with a Spot.

Tea at Upton Cerney was plentiful but informal. People collected tea and food and sat where they pleased. Joel Hegarty rushed out to feed his wife and family and then rushed back to socialize with the opposition. Never easy with small talk, he asked Frank Wall if he had seen any good crop circles lately. Frank (an electrical engineer by trade) said none. Pat Hobby planted himself beside Arthur Fraser and began to 'pitch' him a screenplay called Dead Right, which was perfect for television and could be the pilot for a great Mega-TV series. Arthur, too polite to dash for his Mercedes, closed his eyes and thought of income.

Antony introduced Stephen to several Frenetics he had not really met. John Morrow's eyes lit up when Stephen praised his son's fielding; the boy was fascinated by his camera and seemed to know a great deal of photo-jargon.

Stephen promised them both copies of any decent prints. He discovered with surprise that he had shot off three complete rolls of film and the match was only half finished.

The man with the faraway look, introduced as Jim Wyatt, startled him by greeting him fluently in a foreign language. He talked briefly to the Bramleys and flashed a glance of understanding at Antony. The couple madly in love with each other (Luke and Laura Marriott) gave him a card offering him a free laundry service in any one of twelve British cities. The small lean man (Edward Shaw) excused himself to pad up and open the Frenetic innings.

Frank Wall assembled his team for the field. He asked Joel to supply a Frenetic as umpire to accompany the ancient. Arthur Fraser leapt up to oblige and Pat Hobby, not for the first time, failed to complete a 'pitch' for a screenplay.

Stephen returned to the scorebox with Antony. He watched Edward Shaw advance towards the wicket and was surprised to see him lay down his bat and begin to shadow-box against a tree. 'He does that every match to psych himself up,' Antony explained. 'It reminds him that he is still the undisputed champion of the world.'

But for one small thing Edward Shaw would have been reasonably happy at Upvern School. That small thing was himself. His body refused to grow. It was perfectly healthy, even fit. But it obstinately decided to mark time before puberty. There were no spots on his face. Day by day he pined for them in the mirror, but none ever came. His voice refused to break: mercifully he was tone-deaf and spared the indignity of singing treble in the choir. And he was small.

He coped easily with his work, obtained 9 O Levels and passed safely into the Higher School. He enjoyed cricket and tennis and made good use of the Art School. He served with distinction as a junior committee member of the Debating Society. He was regarded as a most promising boy by seniors and masters and an early candidate to become a study-master. But what use were any of these things when, on his sixteenth birthday, he was barely five feet tall?

At his size Edward knew that he was lucky to be a member of the Garth House at Upvern. At any of the other eight houses (especially the Minster) he would have faced cruel teasing if not actual bullying. But the Garth was notoriously a 'slack' house. It chose not to persecute minorities, especially those made minor for reasons beyond their control.

Edward was duly grateful to the Garth, and revered his housemaster, Mr Fish, a benign soul with a reputation for 'Fishisms' (such as 'What's your first name, Edward?') But the Garth could not stop Edward from resenting his body. Because of his size he felt sure that none of his contemporaries took him seriously or expected him to achieve anything. He would never have a following, nor any reputation except for being small. Above all, his size would never let him be like Russell or Markham.

Paul Russell and Charles Markham had arrived at the Garth with him. He had accompanied them through the school and they were now together in the History Fifth, where Russell and Markham took it in turns to occupy first place (Edward's summit was sixth, out of 17).

Russell and Markham were of average height, good-looking and (when they chose to be) athletic. Russell was a non-stop talker and a wicked mimic. Markham could hear any tune once and repeat it instantly on the Garth house piano. These estimable qualities mattered little to Edward. He admired, almost worshipped, Russell and Markham because from their first day at Upvern they had lived dangerously.

They had refused to stand up when Sixth formers entered their study. They had walked on lawns reserved for prefects. They had worn narrow trousers and wide ties, a precise reversal of the school uniform rules, and their hair had constantly eluded the school barber, Mr Walt (who had learnt his trade on National Servicemen).

Having miraculously survived their first two years, helped by their skill at football, they had now become local legends and had privileges to match. On cold days they invariably persuaded Matron to put them off-games. They played squash together rather than cheer the school in the big match against Malton. In the cadet corps they fainted regularly on Field Days. They acquired an adoring retinue of smaller boys, and allowed the pretty ones to be cheeky. But they had also been seen arm in arm with a girl in the High Street.

Lately they had taken to breaking out of the house at night. They had found a secret place, just for the two of them, and smoked there—not any old cigarettes but Turkish ones. They also experimented with cocktails and something Russell claimed to be cannabis but which failed to ignite. They were a thoroughly bad influence and Edward hung on their every word. He was amazed that they seemed to like him. Heaven smiled when they laughed at one of his jokes or borrowed his history homework. At such moments he dreamt that they might take him to their secret place and offer him Turkish cigarettes.

For generations there had been a feud at Upvern between the Garth house and the Minster. The Minster had always been a 'keen' house but keenness had turned to mania under its present housemaster, Mr Grantham, a man detested by everyone outside the Minster. Even kindly Mr Fish loathed his colleague, who greeted him daily with the same joke: 'Hullo Fish, where's Chips?' Lately Grantham had annoyed him further by urging him incessantly to beat Russell and Markham.

Grantham was obsessed by winning sporting trophies for his house. He knew the name of every promising sportsman at the prep schools which fed Upvern and lured the best into his house year after year. He made Minster boys run a mile each morning while Garthites were still slug-a-beds. Minister boys entered every voluntary sports contest. Minster boys even practised cheering for each other after prayers.

This regime produced results. Minster house regularly won every Upvern sporting cup apart from chess.

Spring term provided a break from Upvern's major sports. The boys did cross-country and athletics, and later in the term there was a voluntary school boxing contest in three sections, Junior, Middle and Senior, divided by weight.

On a bitterly cold day in the first week, Russell and Markham as usual got Matron to put them off games. (Markham was a little disappointed that she did not give him the chance to run one of his famous fevers).

They watched the rest of the Garth house change into shorts and vests for a compulsory school cross-country and gave some encouraging words to their favoured juniors. Then, swaddled in sweaters, scarves and great-coats, they ambled to the Library. Mr Grantham intercepted them and demanded an explanation for their non-running.

'Off games, sir.'

'Of course. Silly me. I forgot that girls don't have games in the Garth.' The master cackled and strutted off.

'Thou art the foul fiend Flippertigibbet,' declaimed Russell, while Grantham was still in range.

'What was that?'

'Shakespeare, sir. King Lear, as a matter of fact. Our English prep. We have Shakespeare in the Upper Fifth.'

Grantham's teaching was confined to the Lower School. He knew that Russell was being insolent but that he could never persuade that fool Fish. Baulked and baffled the beak strode in the direction of away.

Russell and Markham settled into the best chairs in the Library. Markham extracted the latest number of Health And Efficiency from his great-coat. Russell boredly flicked through an old bound volume of the Upvernian.

'Bloody hell, they had a Grantham on the staff in 1894.'

'Poor bastards.'

'Minster won all the medals in the boxing. Except one.

Middles Under Six Stone Four Division, winner E St Q Gumbrill, the Garth.'

'Gumbrill, Gumbrill, yeah, yeah, yeah! Middles Under Six Four? That can't be right. How much do you weigh?'

'Nine-seven.'

'I'm nine-ten and we're not fat. No Middle could be under six-four.'

'It's true. Look, there was a winner in 1895. Another Gumbrill, M St Q, also in the Garth.'

'Must have been a family of midgets.'

Russell scanned more volumes. 'It was contested right up until 1907. Last winner, A McManus, Minster. They've probably kept the medal ever since.'

They sat in silence for a while and then Markham said 'Have you had the same brilliant idea that I've had?'

They found Edward Shaw in his study eating a well-deserved cream bun after a grimly-endured cross-country. 'I'd better have that,' said Markham, grabbing the bun. 'You're getting podgy.'

'Are you mad?'

'Definitely podgy,' said Russell. 'I saw him on the cross-country. He needs a bra under that T-shirt.'

'Piss off.'

'Double pax, Shaw, old bean, old chum, and I'll do your French for a week. But tell me, are you sixteen?'

'Yes.'

'Brilliant. He's a Middle. And how much do you weigh, old sport?'

'Six stone seven,' said Edward miserably.

'Our hero!'

The dangerous pair lifted him onto their shoulders and did a wild lap of honour round the study. 'If you gave up buns do you think you could lose four pounds by the end of February?'

'I don't want to.'

'But then you could enter the Middle Boxing contest in the Under Six Stone Four division and win a medal.'

'I don't want to.'

'But you would not have to. There's no one else like you ... I mean, you would get a walkover.'

'Look,' said Markham. 'The division hasn't been contested since 1907. We've checked. The last winner was in the Minster and they've kept the medal for years. If you entered, that frightful shit Grantham would have to give it to you. It would be a tremendous score for the Garth.'

'Think of good old Fishy.'

Edward was unmoved.

'We'll do your French for the rest of term.' Edward was still unmoved.

Then Markham had an inspiration. 'My mother put on weight when she stopped smoking. So if he's going to lose weight we had better make sure that he smokes, regularly.'

The next day E L Shaw, from the Garth, signed up as a contestant for the Middle Boxing. Mr Grantham thought it a huge joke and tried kindly to make him withdraw. But backed by his trusty seconds Edward stayed firm. Baulked and baffled again, the beak stumped away and consulted the rule book.

Edward had a happy week. He was a hero to the Garth. Mr Fish beamed on him and even remembered his first name. Best of all, he became inseparable from Russell and Markham.

They monitored his caloric intake. They yanked him away from the school tuck shop and dashed doughnuts from his lips. To prevent undesirable muscle gains they persuaded Matron to put him off games (Russell taught him how to stage fits and Markham let him into the secret of running a high temperature). And at night they made him their first-ever guest at their secret place, and gave him Turkish cigarettes. They made him dizzy and sick, but he was having the time of his life.

It was too good to last. The three were in Russell's study one afternoon (off games again) when in burst a junior boy called Linder. He was pretty and knew it, one of those allowed to be cheeky. 'News! News! News!' It was evidently so urgent that he wore running kit to deliver it. Linder paused for effect and took the chance to inspect first his hair then his legs in the mirror.

'Impart!'

'Will you take me to the secret place if I do?'

'You shall be whipped, sirrah.'

'Somebody's put his name down to fight Shaw. A new bug.'

'Liar and slave!'

'It's true, Markham.' The three swept him aside to inspect the school notice-board. Linder trotted after. 'Can I have a fag? Will you mix me a cocktail? Take me to the secret place...'

On the notice-board they saw a strange signature under Edward's: K Chungkalorn, the Minster. 'They say he's mad,' said Linder.

The next day the Upper Fifth had a new member, an Oriental boy. He was two inches shorter than Edward but looked very fit. This was confirmed by his first cross-country run. Everything there was of him was muscle and bone. In afternoon class the master could not open his cupboard door; the new boy smashed through the heavy panel with his fist. This was K Chungkalorn, Edward's opponent. But what was he doing in the Minster?

Enlightenment came from Preston. Although a member of the Minster he was a decent sort of egg. As the master droned Preston whispered to Russell 'He's a Thai. He's some kind of prince. He got expelled from Eton. Grantham said he could come to the Minster.'

'Why did he get expelled?'

'He broke another boy's jaw and left him unconscious for two days.'

That evening Edward said, 'I'm not fighting him. He'll kill me.'

Russell tried to rally him. 'Play the man, Master Shaw! You get two points for the house just for getting into the ring and fainting with terror.'

'You'll have to train,' said Markham. They took him to the Garth house boxing practice. 'Linder, you're a little weed, go and spar with Shaw.' Linder pouted, tossed his head and swung a puny arm. Edward was knocked insensible.

Linder strutted through the count. When he recovered Edward pleaded for withdrawal. Ruthlessly his seconds refused to hear of it.

'That cheat Grantham,' said Markham. 'You can't let him get away with importing a ringer.'

'Fear not,' said Russell. 'Plots have I laid, inductions dangerous.'

The next day Russell summoned another of their junior vassals. 'Fitzmaurice, has Linder been swanking over knocking out Shaw?'

'You bet.'

'Do they know about it in the Cloister?'

'You bet.'

'Brilliant. Take this pound, go to Cloister house and find Melbury and bet on Shaw against Chungkalorn. Hold out for a hundred to one against. Ante-post.'

'You bet,' said Fitzmaurice, who aspired to wit.

It was never difficult to find Melbury of the Cloister house. A pale, bespectacled, unctuous boy, he had set up two years before as school bookmaker. He had two large attendants called Crayford and McVitie, for protection and collection. He was puzzled by Fitzmaurice's bet. But business was slack and if people wanted to throw away a pound on a no-hoper who was he to refuse?

Edward's form in training continued to disappoint. Linder knocked him down several times and was withdrawn as sparring partner in favour of Matron's teddy bear. In their first bout, Edward slipped and hurt his knee too badly to continue, thus becoming the first-ever victim of a technical knock-out by a teddy bear.

'Don't worry,' said Russell. 'So long as you make the weight.'

Russell's plot was ludicrously simple. 'Chungkalorn, old bean, friend of my youth. You look famished. Come to the tuck shop.'

But Chungkalorn refused politely. Markham had no better success with his offers of pies, cakes and ice creams. The pair tried to arouse the Thai contender's appetite by guzzling huge feeds in his sight. But this too failed: they each acquired an extra chin but Chungkalorn stayed slim.

Russell sought an ally in the enemy stable. He persuaded Preston to bet on Shaw at a hundred to one, using Walters, another favoured Garth junior, as intermediary to deceive Melbury. Sure enough, the school bookmaker smelled no rat, only another sucker.

In the Minster house Preston offered every known form of starch, carbohydrate and poly-saturated fat to his new chum Chungkalorn. The Thai boy refused them all. He continued to terrorize his sparring partners. And all the while the weigh-in was getting closer.

The Garth's champion and his seconds were close to despair, but Preston brought a ray of hope. 'Chungkalorn accepted one of my chocolate assortment.'

'Which one?'

'I didn't see.'

'You frabjous ass! Buy the same box and leave it in front of him and don't let anyone else get near it,' ordered Russell.

'Easier said than done. Grantham's set spies on him. So has Melbury. They know someone's trying to nobble him.'

However, a few hours later Preston was back. 'It was definitely the pistachio marzipan.' Markham at once bicycled to the nearby town of Stonehaven (famous for whelks and blankets). He emptied every sweet-shop of its stock of pistachio marzipan chocolates and then repeated the operation in the neighbouring town of Magden (cow heels and pillowcases).

He and Russell had no chance to offer Chungkalorn the chocolates in school. They could see him being watched by Melbury's goons. So they transferred them to Preston, for administration in the Minster. He was their last hope.

'News! News! News!' Linder again burst into Russell's study and preened before the mirror. 'Grantham caught Preston and Chungkalorn eating chocolates and he beat them both and confiscated the chocs! Can I have some vodka, Markham? How about a fag? Take me to the secret place?' They chased him away but with no enthusiasm. They felt dished and dashed, diddled and done.

The chums broke the news to Edward after boxing practice, where he had performed as hopelessly as ever and hurt his hand badly on the punch bag. 'I say, Edward.' Russell's use of the first name made him jump. 'You really don't have to fight him. It's perfectly all right if you pull out.'

'I'm not pulling out. What sort of man would beat a boy for eating chocolates?' Russell and Markham looked at him. Then together they raised his arms high and posed for the invisible photographers.

That night Russell was woken from a deep sleep by someone shaking him.

'Buzz off, Linder,' he mumbled without opening an eye.

'It's not Linder, it's me, Preston.'

Russell was wide awake. 'Preston! How did you get in?'

'Ssh. Through the front door. You're such a slack house you never lock up properly. Suppose I was a mass murderer… Listen, are you and Markham breaking out tonight?'

'No. We're having a rest.'

'Well, could you? I've got Chungkalorn outside.'

'Chungkalorn?'

'Ssh. Yes. Get up and see him. We can't talk here. It's important. He wants revenge on Grantham. Wake up Markham, and we'll tell you all about it.'

'Meet me in our changing room in two minutes.' Russell was out of bed and through the bathroom window in a flash. He shimmied up the drainpipe and oozed into Markham's dormitory. He shook his chum hard.

'Not tonight, Linder,' mumbled Markham.

'Ass. It's me. Changing room. Now.'

Soon they were in the Garth changing room, piling on other boys' clothes.

'Help yourself, Preston,' said Russell affably, passing him the Head of House's tracksuit. 'You too, Chungkalorn old bean, you must be frozen. By the way, do you mind if Shaw joins us?'

'Of course not,' said Preston. 'In fact he should.' Markham brought Edward down. When the five had finished clothing themselves Preston resumed.

'Listen, Chungkalorn wants revenge. He was planning to go and scratch from the boxing but I told him Grantham would be down on him like a ton of shit and that it would be much more subtle if he got too fat for the weigh-in like we planned only I'm flat broke and I can't afford to feed him and I thought you chaps could provide the food only it's no use giving it to me because there are spies and thought police all over the Minster and so we came here because we thought you'd have a wheeze.'

'You did right, Preston. Now if you gentlemen will excuse us, we shall return with food and take you to our private dining room.'

The three Garthites raided every open larder and tuck box in the house. Necessity owes no law. Presently they led the other two into the chill night air.

To this day none of the five has ever revealed the location

of the secret place. All that is known is that it lay some ten minutes' trot away from the back door of the Garth.

Once inside the five friends clasped hands and Russell said 'Liberty.'

'Liberty,' said Markham.

'Liberty,' said Edward.

'Liberty,' said Preston.

'Liberty,' said Chungkalorn.

Then Russell said 'Against tyranny all forms of resistance are legitimate. Kukrit Chungkalorn, make this chocolate cake your burning spear.'

'God, I'm hungry,' said the Thai boy, forlornly. While the others smoked (Turkish, of course) Chungkalorn ate and ate. He ate to protest against injustice, he ate again to celebrate the end of loneliness, the discovery of friends. At last he stopped. The five clasped hands again and intoned the word 'Liberty.'

'Same time tomorrow? Can you chaps break out of the Minster again? I tell you what, why don't you both get a spell in the San, it's much easier to get in and out and you'll be out of reach of the thought police? Charles here will teach you how to get scarlet fever. He's a scarlet fever specialist.'

So Preston and Chungkalorn caught scarlet fever from Markham and were sent to the sanatorium (which had the advantage of keeping Chungkalorn off cross-country and boxing training). Every night they joined the Garthites at the secret place, and Chungkalorn ate and ate.

Just before the weigh-in he and Preston pronounced themselves cured and walked out of the San. At the weigh-in, conducted fussily by Mr Grantham, Edward was skeletal. He made the weight with pounds to spare.

Chungkalorn mounted the scales and stared Mr Grantham in the face. Then he removed his loose tracksuit. He had turned into a pocket Michelin man. Tyres of triumphant flesh cascaded over his shorts. A furious Grantham piled weights on the scale. Baulked and baffled again, he surrendered to his foes

E L Shaw (the Garth) had achieved a walk-over in the Middle Boxing (Under Six Stone Four Division). There was a commotion. Melbury, the school bookmaker, had fainted.

A few days later Edward received his championship medal from a glowering Grantham, to long applause. It was very dusty. Linder boasted that he could knock out the champion any time.

Russell and Preston presented their proxies' betting slips to a snivelling Melbury. They collected forty pounds each and a postdated cheque. It was enough for two feasts, one private, one public. The private feast, for the secret five only, was held in a new restaurant in Stonehaven. It served Thai food.

Then Russell treated the whole of the Garth house to a monster feed. But everyone knew they owed it to Edward. He was taken very seriously indeed. And that night he saw a wondrous thing on his face in Russell's mirror. His first spot.

'That was it, really,' said Antony Scorer. 'Edward Shaw retired undefeated from the ring. He is still the undisputed champion of the world. Immediately afterwards he started to grow. The next cricket season he made the Upvern second team and the year after he was in the first. As an opener. He's in Wisden. Average 28.67, highest score 82 not out. But it was the boxing which opened up his life, made him believe in himself. I'm sure I don't need to tell you that it wasn't winning the medal...'

'No,' broke in Stephen. 'The victory was deciding to fight when Russell and Markham said he could pull out. Do you know what happened to them?'

'Markham's a jazz pianist. He lives with Linder, who's an actor. Usually macho tough guys. They've been together for over ten years. Melbury became a clergyman. He preaches hell-fire sermons on the evils of gambling. Edward has his own business. Art supplies. I do the accounts. It is … not a *small* business. Chungkalorn went back to Thailand at the end of that term at Upvern. He's now a lawyer, specializing in human rights.'

'Good lord. I've met him. Big fat chap. You still haven't told me about Russell.'

'It's too sad. He became a frightfully stuffy Tory MP. Very strong on law and order and morality. He made a big speech against lowering the age of homosexual consent.'

Air Letter

Edward Shaw's opening partner was Alan Harper. His preparations for the innings consisted of kissing his wife and glowering at the rest of the world.

The McFarland brothers opened the Upton Cerney attack. Jess, the elder, showed no fatigue after his long innings and Nat, the younger, had something to prove after his cheap dismissal. Both were fast and Nat hit the Spot several times. Frank Wall set a very attacking field.

The two batsmen had contrasting styles. Edward Shaw was very correct. After two overs of watchful defence he allowed himself to cut two fours in succession just backward of square.

Alan Harper's method was to glower even more intensely at the cosmos and then lurch forward. Occasionally, for variation, he swung his bat through the line of the ball. During the opening spell he received most of the bowling at the Spot end, and was hit several times on the body. He also achieved five fours, three over the bowler's head and two over the wicketkeeper's.

After eight overs the Frenetics had reached 38 without loss. Frank Wall replaced the elder McFarland with Turner, the well-named spinner. His first ball was a hanging full toss to Alan Harper, who swiped it straight to mid-wicket. He retired glowering mightily and cursing himself.

'They got him out that way last year and the year before that,' commented Antony Scorer, after a glimpse through his beautiful books.

The next batsman was the boyish wicketkeeper. In a

Christopher Robin sun-hat he looked barely older than Tim Morrow. 'New player?' asked Stephen.

Antony smiled. 'How old would you say Joe Barnes is?'

'Early twenties?'

'He's thirty-seven. But you're right in a way. He's still living in his early twenties.'

'What does he do?'

'He writes advertising, and very successfully. Do you know this? "It beams… it gleams… it's much more than it seems… it adds a certain lustre to the duster of your dreams…"'

Stephen picked up the rest of the jingle. '"It flows … it glows… smells mighty like a rose… does all the good it could for wood and leaves a shine that shows…" I heard the Shimmer Wax jingle in Hyderabad. He wrote it? I hope he made a lot of money.'

'He did. But he spent a lot, too, living in his early twenties the whole time. He blew a lot when he went to Hollywood to become a famous screenwriter.'

'Like Pat Hobby?'

'I've seen two screenplays of Joe's. They seemed pretty good to me. Actually Joe is in awe of Pat, because he's got credits, even though he hasn't sold anything for years. Anyway, Joe took off to Hollywood a few years ago and it very nearly brought him to his senses. He almost made the best decision of his life. But he used the wrong stationery.'

'Once again, you intrigue me.'

'For years Joe had an on-off relationship with a lady called Emma Tarlow. She was very attractive, very smart and what Americans call a "structured" person and Joe should have married her. But Joe wasn't mature enough to take that decision. He would make a big joke of it—"nobody should marry wicketkeepers, they're all mad"—but he really could not handle a big decision like that, and every time they got close to marriage Joe would run away.

I mean, literally, he would skip off to another country and come back when he'd run out of money.

'Emma could not wait for ever for him to grow up. Finally she really put him on the spot, and Joe ran away as usual. He decided to go to Hollywood and become a famous screenwriter. At that point she told him she was going to marry someone else, a mature man who didn't play cricket, or write, or run away when it mattered.

'That very nearly made Joe grow up. He came very close to saying what they both needed. But he chose the wrong stationery.'

He stared for five minutes at the air letter in the typewriter. It stared back at him, blue and blank and mocking, until he could take it no longer and he went back to the window and watched the sun setting over West Hollywood.

He paced the room a few times, then returned to the typewriter and reversed the air letter. He found the address line and typed in 'Miss Emma Tarlow, 17a Barford Court, London SW6, England.' Then he reversed the air letter again, put it back into the typewriter and lined up the edges.

It seemed to him that American air letters had a bigger space for a message than English ones.

In a burst of creativity he typed in his address: 'c/o McGrory, 5378 Culloden Way, Hollywood, California 90068, USA.' That occupied four whole lines. His fingers hovered over 213 for the telephone area code, then swerved away. Better for her not to telephone, and he knew the McGrorys had an unlisted number.

But he was able to use up two more lines on the date. He forced himself to write it American-style: February 27. He left a big blank space to write 'Dear Emma' by hand. This took him a third of the way down the first page of the air letter before having to start the message. He thought for a moment of switching to double spacing.

Not fair. This letter means a lot to Emma. The least I can do for her is single-space typing.

Quickly he typed 'Thank you so much for your letter and the wedding incitation.' He looked at the last word and laughed bitterly.

Freudian typing error. He changed the c to a v.

'I am afraid that they only caught up with me today, because as you can see from the above address, I have moved on from New York.'

New paragraph.

'I have been staying in Hollywood with my friends the Magrories (Stephanie and Frank) whom you will remember from last year when they came over to London.' *Another three lines used up.* 'They are a riot—as you will also remember!!'

Two exclamation marks to make them a shared joke. 'Stop if you heard this one last year. Guy needs a heart transplant. Surgeon offers him a choice of hearts, one from a 20-year-old marathon runner, the other from a 60-year-old Hollywood agent. Guy says he'll take the agent's, surgeon says why, guy says he'd like one that hasn't been used!!' *Great joke and a lot more space filled.*

'From my window I can see the sunset over the Boulevard which gives it its name'. *Ho-ho and more space.*

'I can also see the lovely homes of several dozen famous movie and TV stars.' *I nearly sent you one of those maps of stars' homes for you to smile over, but you aren't allowed to enclose anything in an air letter.*

'I have been in Hollywood for just ten days and I have become an overnight nonentity'

Ho-ho, but careful, I daren't make this too downbeat.

'Seriously, it's all really great and I feel good about myself as the natives say hereabouts.' *Good. Almost onto page 2 and I haven't even talked about the weather yet.*

'It's partly the weather, which is absolutely terrific. High 70s, fabulous skies (even the smog is technicolour), real sun. Actually, a fatal climate for me, it just makes me think I'm on holiday.' *Careful, I spent my last holiday with Emma. Don't let me remember what she said on our last night.*

'I just can't sit down and do any work.'

New paragraph. Great. This one will carry me into page 2. This is going more easily than I thought. 'Unfair. That is in fact a libel on myself. I have been working up a storm. I'm into a thing— that's very Californian, being "into" things, called Killer With Style which is positively the best screenplay what I have written this week. It is my ninth screenplay since Christmas. I am becoming the Ernie Wise of motion pictures!' *Exclamation mark just in case she takes that seriously. She always felt sorry for Ern.*

He looked down at the typewriter. *I've crossed the frontier into page 2. Dare I use up another ten lines and tell her the plot of Killer With Style? Or will that remind her of too many evenings in the San Carlo listening to my newest plot? Dammit, here goes. This letter would not be from me without my latest masterpiece in it.* 'Killer With Style is about this hack writer who runs this correspondence school for writers. He never sees the students, he teaches them by mail.

'All the students are terrible, but one day he gets a brilliant manuscript by a new student—under an obvious pseudonym. The manuscript has a description of a murder. Our hero criticizes it and waits for the next one. Then week after week manuscripts arrive from the new student. They always follow a pattern, one week there is a long description of a victim, the next week the victim's violent death.

'Then one week there is a news story about a violent killing which is exactly like one in the manuscripts by the new student—and our hero realizes that he has been teaching a real killer. But the police don't believe him (because they never do in movies) so our hero turns detective and traces the killer in the only way he can, by literary criticism, slogging through all the killer's manuscripts and finding clues in the text. Finally the killer comes face to face with the hero and makes him read a new manuscript at gunpoint—his own death. The hero escapes in the only way possible—he criticizes the manuscript, only this time he tears it to shreds and the killer-writer goes to pieces and the hero overpowers him.'

Emma will love that plot, she did English at college. And it has used up a huge chunk of blue air letter.

'Californians are very strange people and do everything very peculiarly. I'd be suffering from culture shock if they had any culture. They smile a great deal and seem to mean it when they wish you a nice day. They take ages to say anything and you're not sure if they have said anything when they've said it. They have invented a curious new tense for their verbs, the future indefinite, to be about to be getting one's head (or act) together to do something.' *Again she'll enjoy that bit of language study and again it has filled the blue.*

'Californians are obsessed with their health and self-improvement—mine too, worse luck. I have had a gut full of bran and offers of therapy. I wish we could sneak off again together for fish and chips. I miss you'

He stopped dead and stared at the air letter for a long time, and then very firmly added an r to 'you' and then the word 'cooking'. Then he typed 'I also miss cricket, but that can be remedied. They play it here. The Hollywood Cricket Club is famous for Ronald Colman and David Niven and now me!' *Another exclamation mark for cheer.*

He hit the carriage return. *Page 2 complete. Over the page and only a bit more to fill the Additional Message Area.* 'I have rented a terrible cheap jalopy, but it goes and I bomb up and down the freeways with Steve Winwood on full blast on the stereo. I am going to Las Vegas next weekend and the size of your wedding present will tell you whether my blackjack system works.'

He looked out of the window again. It was now pitch dark. He looked back at the air letter. There was only a little space left. *Leave a gap for a big scrawly signature and I can write the hard bit in just a few lines.*

New paragraph.

'I am so sorry I cannot come to your wedding, but I will still be here in April. I am certain that you and Martin will have a wonderful marriage. He is a great chap. You must both come over here for a second honeymoon— when I am a famous screenwriter with my own pool!!' *Two exclamation marks for an upbeat ending.*

'With love from Tinseltown', then a thick-nibbed signature: Joe.

He shut his eyes and lay back in the chair for some time. Joe re-read the air letter. He made no changes, sealed it, and walked into the night to mail it.

It's a nice letter. I hope it will give Emma a good memory of me. And I hope she will never know why I used an air letter. Because I didn't trust myself to stick ordinary paper into the typewriter. On ordinary paper I might have said that I loved her and that I could not bear to be away from her. And I might have told her that Hollywood was a big mistake, a silly fantasy, and that I belonged with her, and that I would make her happy, and I might have begged her not to marry Martin, and told her that I was coming back to London ... But once I had told the joke, and dealt with the weather and my newest plot and the colourful natives, I knew I wouldn't have space for any of that on an air letter.

'When Emma got that letter she gave up on Joe and married Martin. She told me later that she knew that Joe had run away again, without even opening it. The stationery told her everything...' Antony broke off to record the dismissal of Edward Shaw, caught at cover off Nat McFarland, with the score on 49. 'Number four is Jim Wyatt,' he continued, for the benefit of Stephen and Sam, as the man with the faraway look drifted slowly to the wicket.

Joe Barnes, a stylish but fidgety batsman, almost ran him out with a daft single to post the fifty.

'Joe never made it in Hollywood. He came back to England and wrote advertising again. His screenplays are in a drawer... all but one. Did you notice that he and Pat Hobby have both written a screenplay called Killer With Style?'

'Coincidence?'

'Not exactly. Joe made the mistake of sending a copy of his original screenplay, Killer With Style, to Pat Hobby, for advice. Pat has never believed in wasting good material.'

Stephen watched Frank Wall relieve the younger McFarland with the elder. Turner still wheeled away at the other end. 'Has Joe got a new girl friend?'

'No. Deliberately. He has never forgiven himself for throwing Emma away. As a kind of spiritual hair shirt he carries a blank air letter with him in his wallet. He says people only deserve one chance in life.'

As if to demonstrate this philosophy Joe Barnes got a fine edge to the red-faced wicketkeeper and instantly walked to the pavilion, sparing umpire Fraser the need to judge the appeal. The Frenetics were now 67 for 3.

The Tiger Will Bite Your Legs

'Take a lot of pictures,' said Antony Scorer. 'This is our best batsman.'

It was Luke Marriott, the man with the happy marriage and the laundry van.

But before Stephen could photograph him, the third ball he received from Jess McFarland hit the Spot, reared, and smashed into his left hand. He dropped his bat and tore off his glove (decayed Frenetic stock which had offered little protection). The fielders clustered round making futile suggestions.

John Morrow watched the incident anxiously. He had been bowling to his son, who was padded and ready to go in.

'Put on your helmet, please.'

'I'm all right, Dad.'

'Please.'

'It gives me a headache.'

'Not half as big a headache as a fractured skull and a brain hemorrhage. Fast bowler, dodgy wicket, it's common sense. No one thinks you're a scaredy-cat.'

'All right.' Tim put on the helmet. His father fussed with the straps. By this time Luke Marriott had discovered that he could not grip the bat at all with his bad hand. He retired hurt, with the score still 67.

'I'm in, Dad.'

'Watch the ball. Don't take your eye off when it bounces. Watch. Play yourself in. You don't have to score off the first ball. Remember the tiger...'

But Tim heard none of this. Stephen watched him stride

out to the wicket, a lot more energetically than the dreamy Jim Wyatt. 'Is Tim really your number 6? How old is he?'

'Twelve,' said Antony. 'He should be batting higher. Tim's our little Bradman.'

Ignoring his father's good advice Tim aimed an airy cover drive off his first ball. It flew at catching height between first slip and red-faced wicketkeeper, who left it to each other and gifted Tim a single. John was in torment.

'His biggest weakness,' said Antony. 'Someone told him Bradman always scored off his first ball.'

'His father loves him very much.'

'Even more after last year.'

For a long time John Morrow had pretended that he found it impossibly difficult to drive his car to the street where his son and his ex-wife had gone to live.

The street in question was certainly a challenge, which often defeated taxi-drivers: a cul-de-sac guarded from traffic, at the behest of its rich, fashionable residents, by layers of one-way streets and pedestrian zones. But this was not the real reason why John never drove to his son's door on the alternate weekends when he took him out.

The fact was that he could not bear to park his aging car beside the sleek new models of his ex-wife and her new husband. Still less could he bear to step inside their house: so spacious, so tasteful, so inviting, so much better a place for his son to grow up than the one he had provided.

There always seemed to be friends in that house, interesting people, sometimes even a Household Name, the kind of people he had never introduced to Mary when they were married. Whenever he had entered that house all the friends had stopped talking. He had felt them wondering, what was he doing there, had he come to *repair* something? And Mary and Steve had rescued him, *explained* him, but so delicately, so politely…

The politeness was the hardest thing to bear. But then everything had been done so politely, from the day when Steve had joined John's cricket team to the day he had walked away with John's wife and child.

No one could be blamed for the break-up. It was not Steve's fault that he was a better cricketer than John, that he was richer, and funnier, and that he could make people feel happy and interesting. John could no more blame Mary and Tim for turning to Steve than blame a plant for turning from the moon to the sun. But he still could not bear it when they were polite to him.

The divorce had been amicable. She had left him the flat, her share in trust for Tim, and asked for only nominal maintenance. His only child did not need any money from him—or anything else?

He nearly missed Tim, waiting for him on the street corner. But it was him, after all, under the new haircut, leaning on the pastiche Victorian lamp-post with his cricket bag beside him. John pulled abruptly to the left.

The BMW behind called out 'You stupid bastard!' loud enough for his son to hear. He stepped out and declaimed 'Tim Morrow and Tim Morrow and Tim Morrow…'

His son laughed hastily, preventing him from adding 'Creeps on this petty pace from day to day.' He had turned it into a family routine, but he still felt guilty about naming Tim to flatter a childless relative, guiltier still when Great-Uncle Timothy had left nothing in his will to his namesake.

I gave him a joke name for nothing. Does Tim get teased about it at his new school? He should take Steve's name. Tim Sharp. No problems there…

His son accepted a brief hug. 'What have you done to your hair?'

'Not me. Michael. At the Studio. Steve took me there. Michael does Imran Khan!' John looked suitably awestruck. He remembered dragging a protesting Tim down the High Street to ancient Mr Walt (who had butchered Edward

Shaw's hair at Upvern School). The unknown Michael was a wizard. He had given Tim a new face. Suddenly John could see the man waiting inside his eleven-year-old son.

John opened the car door. 'You did not bring a friend?'

'Nobody could come.'

Nobody wanted to come...

'I like it when it's just you and me, Dad.'

I wish I could believe that...

'Can you take me to the nets, Dad? We haven't played cricket for ages.'

John agreed and they drove off.

'How's school?'

'Brilliant!'

Of course it is. And if Steve wants to pay the fees, with no children of his own and with Mary who should not have another, who am I to stand in the way?...

'Do you know about the holidays yet?'

'Steve's doing a shoot in the Indian Ocean but Mum and I can join him and there's a huge beach with coral and things and Steve says I can learn to scuba-dive.'

Yes, I can see that beats driving to my mother's in Hampshire in this clapped-out car...

'How's your swimming?'

'I did a mile in the school Swimathon. Steve takes me a lot.'

Another unintended pill for John to swallow. He remembered his last aquatic outing, with Tim fearful and clinging despite the arm-bands and the rubber ring.

They reached the park with the good cricket nets. For years he had hauled Tim across London to use them. They were the best outdoor nets they knew. More important, they were the place where Tim had played his first real cricket with a hard ball. Moving house had brought him much nearer the 'good' nets, near enough for long evening sessions with Steve. Tim's cricket had improved dramatically.

Suddenly the car was hit by the first of the rain which had threatened all day. They watched the already poor footholds in the nets turn into Passchendaele.

'I suppose this means the Science Museum again.'

Objection, Your Honour. Even Steve cannot stop the rain...

'Not if you don't want to.'

'I didn't mean it that way, Dad. I like the Science Museum. Really.'

Tim did seem to like the Museum, but John had eyes only for the other 'weekend fathers'.

Am I as obvious as they are?...

'Have you heard any more about the new job, Dad?'

'No.' But he had heard. The job was his. Challenge, responsibility, and almost as much money as Steve must earn. But he had not been able to tell Mary or Tim it was in Bahrein. He would not see Tim for ages. That alone had kept him from accepting. He had to let them know on Monday. To change the subject he bought Tim an expensive dinosaur he did not really want.

It was still raining when they left the Museum. A film (John was sure Tim had seen it before) and an indifferent Chinese meal filled up time before the long drive back to the old neighbourhood which Tim had left to his father. Many of the High Street shops were boarded up, but Mr Walt was still there, cutting hair like yesterday.

They had to park some way from the flat. The long side-street was dark and there were several lager louts. Tim reached for his father's hand and held it until the front door was bolted behind them.

That's the first time he's not been bored...

'How about a long bath, PJs on and some gin rummy?'

After flicking through the channels on the old portable television (Steve of course had a satellite dish), Tim agreed.

John listened to his son splash in the bath, pleased to hear him still ready to dive-bomb the old toy boats. Tim returned, squeaky-clean like a child in one of Steve's commercials, wearing some old pyjamas.

They're too small for him. Everything here, everything this weekend, is too small for him…

Their gin rummy was soon interrupted by the Mad Pole, a recent occupant of the flat upstairs. On Saturday nights he got drunk and would deliver a guttural harangue accompanied by breakages. John had turned it into a shared joke, but not enough of a joke for Tim to want to leave his lap in the lighted room.

I bet he's never scared at home. Home… What have I said? But it's true. This isn't home any more…

At last he was able to put his son to bed. Tim dropped several years when he begged John to leave the light on. It revealed cruelly the dreariness of the room, no longer 'Tim's room' but 'the spare room'. All of Tim's cherished possessions had been carted off to Steve's where they had greatly multiplied.

John watched his son start to dream, dreams which other people would make true.

He has no future with me, only a past…

Next morning started brilliantly. Tim woke him with a cup of tea and a big hug. They shared The Mail On Sunday on his bed and Tim recited the cricket scores from memory, just like the old days. Then they had Sunday breakfast—a huge feast of illicit delights which John had fried since time immemorial. Tim mopped up the last egg and sauce, blew out his tummy and played a drum roll, as always.

Suddenly John's guilt returned.

I've made him live in the past again. Will he have to play my little boy for the rest of his life?…

They washed up together and Tim settled into some homework. John could not help him: he had never done Latin. While Tim concentrated John stared at the job offer from Bahrein.

'I'm finished, Dad. Can we play cricket?'

It had turned into a fine Sunday. John made quick time across London to the 'good' nets.

As Tim padded up John noticed his new hand-made Newbery bat, already well marked in the middle. He did not need or want to ask if Steve had supplied it.

John was a probing, accurate bowler, fast by the standards of an eleven-year-old batsman. To his pleasure Tim met each ball unflinchingly, right forward or right back, not attempting anything much but in control. At last his slower ball produced a caught-and-bowled and they changed over.

'You've improved. A lot.'

Tim's bowling was less distinguished. John blocked the better ones and helped himself off the rest. Tim wisely ignored a screaming drive and the ball was fielded for him by a watching Australian.

'I'm going to try something else, Dad.' The first attempt missed the net, but the second produced a delighted squeal for lbw.

'That hit a bump. Anyway, Steve has no right to teach you top-spinners.'

In Tim's second innings his feet really began to dance. John was cut and driven savagely. He speeded up, but Tim remained a half-second ahead of him.

The Australian moved closer to watch. 'Who's batting, Don Bradman?'

'Murdered in broad daylight by my own son.'

My stuff must come easy after Steve's…

John plugged on. An exhausted half-volley was hit miles over his head. 'Six and out. How about a drink?'

'Oh please, Dad. We've still got twenty minutes.'

I bet Steve never gets tired…

'Can I give him a few?' The Australian produced a newish ball from his pocket.

'Not too fast. He's only eleven.'

'I don't mind, Dad.' The Australian ran a few paces and

bowled a ball at the same pace as John's quickest. He obviously had plenty in reserve. Tim watched the first four, again right forward or right back. He straight-drove the fifth, leaving the Australian flat-footed in his follow-through.

He put much more into his next delivery. It was short of a length and flew. But Tim was in position and knocked it down from in front of his throat.

'I said, not fast! Look at the size of him!'

'It's all right, Dad. Really.'

John watched in amazement as Tim and the Australian settled into a duel. Nothing had led him to believe that his eleven-year-old son could cope with a high-quality adult fast bowler on a suspect surface.

Steve really has brought him on…

Tim played an exquisite on-drive and was hopelessly bowled trying to repeat it. He removed gloves, pads and box, and then remembered his manners by inviting the Australian to bat.

'Naah, I'm all right. Who taught you to bat like that?'

Go on. Be truthful. Tell him about Steve, I don't mind…

'My dad taught me. My dad brought me here years ago when I was little and before he started to bowl at me he said that whatever happened I mustn't step back because you can't hit the ball properly if you step back. And my dad said he knew I would be scared of the hard ball so he said he would make me even more scared of stepping back so he reached in his bag and he pulled out a tiger and put it behind my feet and he said "If you step back the tiger will bite your legs." And it was silly because it was only a toy tiger but I didn't want it to bite my legs. And after a while Dad stopped taking the tiger with us but I still think about him when I'm batting and it just sort of works.'

We haven't talked about that for years. But that is exactly what happened…

They said goodbye to the Australian at the drinking

fountain without taking his name or address. They would not matter to John in Bahrein.

Now I can go in peace. I gave my son a good start after all. There are poorer legacies than knowing how to bat. But I have nothing more to give…

'Can we go to the river, Dad?' Another very old stamping-ground but it was Tim's request, unprompted.

In the car Tim said 'Tell me about the job again, Dad?' So he did, but again without mentioning Bahrein. At the river Tim reached into his cricket bag and fished out a camera, an expensive Nikon, Steve's birthday present. 'Can you work this, Dad?'

'I have taken photographs before.' But Tim took him carefully through all the controls.

They followed their usual route. Everything was perfect and as it had always been—the spooky place, and the Tarzan tree, and Rat's home, and the hired rowboat—and Tim insisted they take pictures of each other in each place.

Whom are all these pictures for, him or me? Either way, he must know this is a goodbye…

They had tea by the river and drove to Steve's home. Tim's home. At the usual street corner Tim said 'You've never seen my room, Dad.'

So for once John parked and followed his son home.

Damn it, I would like to picture him in his room when I'm in Bahrein…

Mary and Steve were genuinely delighted to see him, but before John could accept a drink Tim had dragged him to his room. It was airy and left plenty of room for property. John took in the mountain bike, the computer, the stereo and piles of clothes and casual shoes.

Guarding everything from the pillow of the bunk bed was a toy tiger.

'Good grief. Is that Tiger?'

'Yes. Look.' Tim held out the toy without releasing it.

None other. The one who had threatened to bite Tim's legs.

Mary had slipped in. 'Tiger's still the one and only. We had terrible tears last week when Tiger got lost.'

Everyone seemed to want him to stay for supper, so he did.

Back at his flat John wrote 'Dear Mr Al-Tahouni, Thank you so much for your offer, but I fear I must inform you that family commitments make it impossible for me to accept.'

Porto Alegre

Stephen took many pictures of Tim Morrow's innings, thinking that they might be of commercial value in years to come when the boy made it to the England team. After his horrid first-ball whoosh Tim batted beautifully. The invisible tiger was hard at work, propelling his feet into position. He forced both McFarlands and when Turner, the spinner, bowled him his deadly Flighted Ball he skipped down the wicket and drove it through long-on for four.

At the other end Jim Wyatt batted with the same detachment which he had displayed throughout the match. He took ones and twos anonymously but at will. He made no effort to protect his young partner except to take over all responsibility for the calling. He could remember being twelve himself and too shy to order grown-ups about. Their stand prospered.

The Frenetic hundred went up when Jim Wyatt pushed another two past cover. Frank Wall tried some change bowlers, Ray Senior (alleged off breaks), Ted Smith (medium nothings), himself (cutters). The batsmen continued to help themselves. When Antony Scorer acknowledged the call of 'Last twenty overs' from the umpire the Frenetics had victory on a plate.

Finally Frank Wall turned to the cross-grained Custer. Irked at being neglected for so long he began with a ball of great pace. It was a beamer, with no sightscreen behind it, and for the first time Tim was grateful for his helmet. John rushed onto the pitch and all the fielders apologized furiously. Tim was given time to recover, which Jim Wyatt extended by a long re-tying of his bootlaces.

Custer over-compensated for his first ball by bowling a long-hop. Tim instinctively shaped a backward defensive stroke, saw that the delivery was rubbish, changed his mind and dragged the ball onto his stumps.

He had made 31, with four fours. He removed helmet and gloves and walked sadly away. His father gave him a hug and a drink, and Mrs Marriott (the second most beautiful woman in the world) asked him to sit beside her. Tim adored both Marriotts but could never understand why they stayed in the laundry business instead of becoming movie stars. He was shocked at the state of Luke's hand, now swaddled in ice cubes.

The Frenetics were now 126 for 4, effectively for 5 without Luke Marriott. They needed 63 to win with 16 overs left.

Alex Bramley came into bat. He waved at his wife, who waved back as if to a vaguely familiar acquaintance. He took guard to Custer, whose first ball to him hit the Spot, reared, and blooped to first slip off the handle of his bat. He had travelled a long way for a golden duck, but he was still living in an Excellent Moment. The score was now effectively 126 for 6.

Arthur Fraser went to the wicket as the field closed in for Custer's very unlikely hat trick. Arthur was in a black mood. He had needed to think quietly about repairs to Mega-TV's sagging soap opera, The McGintys, but Pat Hobby had wasted all his time trying to sell his wretched screenplay. Custer's bowling was another tiresome interruption. Get away from me, he muttered, as he cross-batted the hat-trick ball through mid-wicket for four.

Jim Wyatt did not like the look of the shot or on Arthur's face. Neither suggested a long innings. He decided to score quickly himself and pinch the strike. For the first time Stephen noticed how good a batsman he was, as he glided down the wicket with the same faraway look on his face.

'Strange man,' he said to Antony. 'Why did he speak to me in Portuguese?'

'Because you've been to Brazil.'

'And has he?'

'There's a story about that.'

The young man dumped his sports bag and leaned against the bus stop. Ahead of him lay the wasteland of Sunday. Wait twenty minutes for the next 19 to take him back to the dark South London bed-sit. Try to avoid the landlady: into his room, decide whether to lie on the bed or sit in the chair. Count his money: Friday's wage packet already half spent on the round of drinks for the football team. Put off phoning his woman for as long as he dared: get his excuses ready...

'Jim! Jim Wyatt!' He looked up at the sound of his name.

'It's really you, Jim.'

He looked into the other man's face. He saw joy, and entreaty, and a hint of puzzlement.

'Frank...' Jim aimed a punch at him with his right. Frank parried but Jim crashed in a left, stopping just short of the unprotected face. 'You still haven't learnt,' said Jim, and he hugged Frank in the rain.

Frank was a year younger but the difference seemed greater. Frank still had an eager, open face, with a big grin, and a sweep of untidy fair hair. The face was sunburnt and the hair bleached. He was beautifully dressed and carried an expensive briefcase. But Jim saw this for only a moment.

He saw him twenty-five years before, the day Frank first moved into the back street of the English provincial town where they grew up. Frank was a skinny boy of seven with long hair, the fairest Jim had ever seen except in films. Jim was nearly nine, the toughest kid on the street, and he was all set to push the new boy around and show him who was boss, but something about Frank made him stop, and for some reason they started playing catch. They did not even have a ball, but threw a stone, a piece of fruit, a used cigarette carton, and then they ran together all over town and back, still playing catch with anything they could lay their hands on.

Then he saw Frank like a series of snapshots, one for almost every good moment of his life for seven years.

This is me and Frank at school. Jim was a year ahead of Frank, and Knew Everything, how to fool the teachers, how to dodge swimming, where to find The Book With All The Answers. Jim protected Frank from the school bullies.

This is me and Frank in the street. Jim told Frank everything about their town, not that there was much— a nowhere place with one cinema and a Third Division football team, a place which famous people were accidentally born in.

But even so it had some worthwhile secrets for its children— houses where spies lived, or murderers, places which supplied cigarettes, ways of getting into the cinema without paying. Jim told Frank every one.

This is me and Frank having a fight. Always pretend, and always 'fixed': Frank would win the early rounds, then Jim would turn on him and compel a submission, then the escape and the chase to the sweet shop.

This is me and Frank playing football. They were both gifted. They always played on the same side. Frank always passed the ball when Jim wanted.

'Frank Harman,' said Jim looking at the gold F H on Frank's briefcase.

'Francisco,' said Frank, but before Jim could pursue the new name the snapshots began again.

This is me and Frank at my house. Not many of these. Jim rarely brought people home to the bachelor uncle who had stepped in out of duty when his parents were killed, and let Jim know it, the uncle who never played football and who gave savings bonds as a birthday present.

This is me and Frank at Frank's house. Frank's parents seemed really old. He had grown-up brothers and sisters. Frank was an afterthought or a mistake. His parents had come down in the world when they moved to Jim's street, and somehow it was Frank's fault.

This is me and Frank where we're not supposed to be.

Most of the snapshots were like that, from their earliest days together. Their school, their town, their lives were too small for them. They had to break away, anywhere, everywhere, so long as it was far or forbidden. This is me and Frank on a homemade raft on the river (neither could swim) ... trying to climb the Town Hall at midnight ... in the shop with the dirty magazines.

They were a perfect team. Jim had the fantastic ideas for things to do. Frank followed fearlessly. And Frank was brilliant at the practical things, bringing the bikes or the torches or the food. And quite often it was Frank who was better at dealing with the unexpected. But Jim always went first.

One snapshot was sharper than the others. *This is me and Frank at the warehouse*. It was their secret place. Long abandoned by commerce, the rotting warehouse by the dirty canal stored their illicit treasures and dreams.

This is me talking about Brazil. Brazil was Jim's idea. It began when he was twelve, Frank eleven. Jim got hold of everything he could about Brazil, even a Teach-Yourself-Portuguese. Jim read aloud by torchlight, while Frank listened. He read about beaches and footballers and music and carnivals, about forests and deserts, about a giant river and jungle cities, about generals and peasants and priests of God and voodoo, about cowboys and cattle, about Indians who had never seen fire or metal. He read about piranhas and alligators and giant sloths and anacondas and lizards and armadillos and coal-black panthers with blazing eyes, and vultures and macaws and humming-birds.

As they grew older Jim read about other things: ports and cities and shanties, giant farms and plantations, about coffee, rubber, sugar, all manner of wood and spices, about colossal mines filled with metals and gold and precious gems, about an ocean of oil, an endless stream of discovery, wealth and power, about sudden fortune and sudden ruin, about beautiful women and desperate men. When he ran out of other things to read about, Jim would simply recite the place names from their school atlas: Pernambuco, Belem, Bahia, Rio Grande del Sud, Porto Alegre…

Of course Jim and Frank were going to Brazil. It would be their ultimate break-out, escape from the drab town and the boring school and the loveless homes and the future.

'If we don't go to Brazil,' said Jim, 'Nothing's going to happen, ever. But we can't miss in Brazil. We'll get a trial at one of the football clubs. We'll do something. You'll see…' He looked across at Frank's face, wide-eyed and faraway.

'Yeah.'

They agreed that as usual Jim would go first. He was older and taller and could pass for more than his age of fifteen. Jim would hitch to London and find the docks and a ship to Brazil and work his passage over and find a job and a place to live and then write to Frank to join him.

The last snapshot came into view. *This is me saying goodbye to Frank*. Frank wanted to come as far as the motorway out of town, but Jim refused and left him in their own street. They had one last pretend-fight and Frank won the early rounds before Jim fought back and pinned him to the ground and promised again to write from Brazil…

'Eighteen years,' said Frank at the bus stop.

'You look flash—and flush,' said Jim, fingering Frank's expensive raincoat.

Frank looked back at Jim. He could not think of a reply

facing Jim's old tracksuit top and threadbare gray trousers.

'I don't care where you're going,' said Frank. 'You're coming back to the flat.' He dragged Jim away from the bus stop.

Jim whistled when he saw the excellent address and gaped when Frank let him into the drawing room. It was the most elegant and comfortable room he had ever seen.

'You… live here, Frank?'

'No, I just use this when I'm in London.'

'Where do you live?'

'In Rio of course.' Frank frowned momentarily and then relaxed.

'You never did get any of my letters, did you? And you never saw my ad in the papers?'

Jim stared at him, mystified. Frank darted to a concealed refrigerator and tossed Jim a chilled can of beer. Jim dropped it.

'Whadda loada rubbish!' Frank was ten years old again.

'You always were a crap goalkeeper. Look, I'm sorry, you come thousands of miles to London and all you get is the same lousy beer we have at home.'

Jim read the name on the beer can: Bramah Chopp, Made In Brazil. Very slowly he asked 'Frank. You live in Brazil?'

'Of course, Jim. The last seventeen years. I went there as soon as I got your postcard.'

Jim watched Frank reach deep into his pocket and extract a postcard. It had been laminated in plastic for protection. Frank handled it like an ikon as he passed it over.

Jim stared at the picture, a view of a bay. He turned it over. The location was unidentified, but there was a big Brazilian stamp with a postmark, on which he read: Porto Alegre. Only then did he look at the message, in his writing, addressed to Frank Harman at their old street. It said

'Brazil is everything we said it would be' and was signed with a big Jim and their secret code-word.

Jim turned it over and over and then handed it back. 'Tell me about it, Frank.'

'Like I say, Jim, as soon as I got your postcard I left town. I was a bit annoyed at you for not putting your address but I reckoned to find you once I got to Brazil. It looked great where you were, it even sounded great. Porto Alegre. I couldn't get over it, not hearing from you for ages and then that postcard from...' He paused, just for the pleasure of saying the name again 'Porto Alegre.

'Anyway, I did what you did, Jim, hitched to London and found a ship, this clapped-out freighter, but it was going to Brazil and they took me on as a deck hand. We landed at Rio and I got past the customs and immigration and there I was in Brazil. I got this job in a cafe, but that was just to get a start. Jim, I did everything we ever talked about doing in Brazil. I even got a trial for Santos; I actually played for Pele's club!'

Frank talked and talked, prompted ceaselessly by Jim. Frank had been all over Brazil. He had worked as a tourist guide, bank manager, journalist, translator, cowboy, archaeologist, plantation overseer, orchid hunter, prospector, actor, racing driver, footballer, bodyguard, gambler, hotel owner, film producer.

'What do you do now, Frank?'

'I've got my own business. Manufacture, construction, import-export, commodities, anything legal I do it. Brazil's a boom and bust place but I can't stop making money. I come to London once a year on business.'

'Do you ever go back to...?' Jim could not bring out the name of their old town. 'No. Never.' Frank's face clouded but instantly lit up again. 'Hell, I haven't told you the greatest thing.' He passed over a snapshot of a beautiful dark-haired woman with an already handsome little boy. 'My wife and son,' he added, unnecessarily.

'We're happy, Jim. All the time. Really. All the time. Like we always said about Brazil, everything turned out right… except…' Suddenly he shook Jim by the shoulders. 'It's bloody fantastic running into you in London of all places. I looked for you all over Brazil. I wrote to you in Porto Alegre, to all the hotels, all the post offices, all the banks. I asked about you everywhere I went, and when I got some money I put ads for you in the papers and I even hired a detective. I couldn't believe you were dead, so I reckoned you must be in trouble with the police or immigration and you didn't want anyone to know you as Jim Wyatt. I had problems too, until the football club sorted them out. Anyway, Jim, what are you doing in London? Do you still live in Porto Alegre?'

'I've never been to Porto Alegre. I've never been to Brazil.'

Frank stepped back.

Jim looked away from him. 'The day I left you I did hitch to London, just like our plan. And I got to the docks and I saw a ship going to Brazil.' He closed his eyes. 'I didn't get on it. I just… lost my nerve. I watched the ship sail away without me. Then I wandered into London and I got a job and a room. A nothing job and a poxy little room. I swore that I'd go back to the docks and get another ship to Brazil. But I never did. Instead I just got another job and another room. It's been that way for years. And that's the way it always will be.'

His voice rose. 'Nothing happened. I never went anywhere. I never did anything. I never married. I never played football for Santos. I play football on Sunday mornings in the bloody park. And it's my fault.' His voice fell again.

'Sorry. Now, Frank, I'll tell you why you got a postcard from me from Porto Alegre.

'I thought about you a lot. After I'd been in London for a year I really wanted to see you or write to you. But I couldn't bear for you to know that I hadn't been to Brazil, hadn't done anything at all. Then one night I met this real live Brazilian in the pub where I was working, and we talked, and he was going back to Brazil in a few days. So I wrote you that postcard and asked him to post it for me in Brazil. It was just a joke, I didn't even know what the picture is, it could be anywhere. I chose the message really carefully. I couldn't bear to lie and say I really was in Brazil, so I wrote something true: "Brazil is everything we said it would be." So… that Brazilian actually posted that card. I'm glad he lived in Porto Alegre. It always was a nice name.'

Jim took a deep swig of Bramah Chopp. 'You shouldn't apologize for the beer, Frank. It's the nearest I'll ever get to Brazil.'

'Not true. I want you to come back to Brazil with me.'

'No chance.'

'You don't know what that postcard did for me, Jim. I nearly went crazy when I didn't hear from you. Stuck in that bloody school, that bloody town, all alone. I had to believe that you'd made it to Brazil. When you didn't write I was sure that you hadn't made it and things like that never happened and you and me would never break out, we were just going to live nowhere, do nothing till we die… Then I got your postcard. So you had made it after all, and I could make it too.'

'Well, now you know that it was a lie.'

'So what? Your postcard gave me my whole life. I owe you one back.' He cleared his throat. 'I want you to come back with me to Brazil.'

'No, Frank.'

'Please, Jim. Your postcard was right, you know. Brazil is everything we said it would be.'

'I'm sure it is. But I can't go there and live off you.'

'I could get you a job, a real job, you wouldn't be taking anything…'

'No. It wouldn't be right. But don't worry, Frank. You've

paid me back already. You say I gave you your life. You've now given my life back to me. Knowing you're in Brazil makes everything all right. That's all that matters to me now. I don't mind the dead-end jobs, the cheap rooms, the women I don't really love. But please write to me every once in a while. From Brazil. And one day, Frank, I promise, you'll get another postcard from me, asking you to pick me up on the waterfront at Porto Alegre.'

Pat Hobby Runs Out Of Luck (reprise)

'That's Jim Wyatt,' said Antony Scorer.

'Another man whose life was changed by stationery. Even though it redeemed his life to know that Frank got to Brazil he is still trying to get there himself. He's learnt Portuguese, he's written to the embassy, Brazilian firms, British firms with Brazilian interests. The problem is that he needs a sponsor and a guaranteed job and he simply won't take anything from Frank. Shot! And that's his fifty!'

With unaccustomed violence Jim had pulled Turner for four. The Frenetics were 154 for 5, de facto for 6. They needed 35 for victory, nine overs left.

The fifty seemed to infect Jim with a terrible fatigue. For the next over he prodded drearily from the crease. At the other end Arthur Fraser was still irritated. He flailed his bat at everything without result. E M Forster's motto flashed into his mind: only connect. It made him more irritated and even less able to hit the ball. Fortunately for him none of the balls he missed were on the wicket.

Jim Wyatt wondered if he should have a word with his partner, and if so, what word, and while still wondering he hit a lacklustre return catch to Frank Wall. He slipped away from the crease, his eyes still looking for Brazil. The Frenetics were now 156 for 6, 33 runs from victory, one batsman injured, and there were seven overs and two balls left.

John Morrow went to the wicket with some helpful instructions from his captain. 'We're still going for the runs if you think we can get them but if you're not going for them shut up shop.' Tim said, encouragingly but inaccurately, "They're rubbish, Dad!'

John was a limited batsman. At the start of each season he eliminated every stroke that had got him out the previous year. There were now only three in his repertoire: forward defence, backward defence, push through the covers.

Don't embarrass Tim... The thought made him still more inhibited. Grimly he guarded his wicket. At the other end Arthur's lunges were still unproductive. The score advanced only by a few thick edges off the returning McFarland brothers.

John snicked a ball just short of slip. He sensed his son's anguish.

This is silly. I might as well give him something to remember... Off Nat McFarland's next ball he unchained his first square cut for twelve years in a competitive match, and watched it skim over the boundary.

So that's what it's like...

He tried to repeat the experience next ball and was caught at gully. The Frenetics were 165 for 7, really for 8, 24 to get off six overs and one ball.

Arthur Fraser's irritation reached new heights when he saw that the next batsman was Pat Hobby, who marched up to him for a mid-wicket conference.

Good God, the fool's still trying to pitch his screenplay...

In fact, Pat had felt it necessary to give a pep talk. 'You're doing great, Arthur, we're going to do it, they're panicking, keep on keeping on...'

Arthur ground several teeth. Pat blocked the last ball of the over and called 'Up to you, Arthur?'

Arthur was now in a foul temper. He played a terrible wahoo at Jess McFarland and the ball shaved his stumps. Got to get down the other end, thought Pat, keep Arthur alive.

Arthur finally connected with his next ball and it

squirted out to cover. Pat started running. 'No!' bellowed Arthur, correctly.

God help me, don't run him out, don't run him out... Pat was still saying 'Don't run him out' to himself when Arthur edged the next ball through the slips, and he was still saying it when he found himself three quarters of the way down the pitch without giving his partner (and prospective customer) any sort of call.

'Aaagh!' screamed Pat, and he turned on his heels, away from Arthur's frozen stare. 'Bowler's end!' he bawled as slip retrieved the ball. Pat was run out by three yards. The Frenetics were 165 for 8, and Luke Marriott's hand was still swollen. 24 still to get, off five overs and three balls.

Joel Hegarty said goodbye to his wife and daughters and marched towards the crease. 'Captain's innings, Joel,' said some fool.

Joel possessed a wide range of handsome shots, but played them in a completely random order. If they matched up to the delivery in question he was likely to score quickly. Otherwise the first straight ball was usually enough. Stephen heard Antony explain this as Joel shouldered arms, with great elegance, to three balls in a row.

Frank Wall brought back Turner to bowl at Arthur Fraser. After watching Arthur's lunges he calculated that the deadly Flighted Ball would soon see him off.

Unfortunately Arthur's temper had improved dramatically with the dismissal of Pat Hobby. He had thought of a new character to revive Megalopolitan's sagging soap opera, The McGintys—a comic-pathetic character perpetually trying to sell rubbish to the rest of the cast. His cares melted away and he remembered how to bat. He met Turner's deadly Flighted Ball with a perfect straight drive for four, and kept the strike with a single. The Frenetics were now 170 for 8 (really for 9). 19 to win, four overs left.

Nat McFarland wasted time re-setting the field, but it

did not break Arthur's good mood. He played two calm backward defensives, then a push past cover.

'Look for two!' But Ray Senior had too good an arm to risk it. Joel had to face the last three. He played a stern forward defence to a long hop, then attempted a late cut to a yorker. To the last ball Joel played his famous cover drive. Luckily it coincided with a half volley on the off stump. The Frenetics reached 175: 14 to win, three overs left, one wicket to fall.

Frank Wall decided not to risk his spinner against the new Arthur, and recalled Jess McFarland. Arthur jabbed down on two fast balls. The next hit the reverse side of the Spot, shot through and trapped Arthur so lbw that Edward Shaw as umpire could not refuse. The Frenetics had lost by 13 runs. Or had they? In the best Boy's Own Paper tradition the injured Luke Marriott was calling for pads and gloves. He tore himself away from his beautiful wife and Stephen photographed them playing out a melodrama.

'No dearest, I beg you.'

'Darling, I must. England needs me.'

Finally she wept pretend tears and gave him her scarf. He kissed it tenderly and wrapped it round his neck.

'Do they always go on like that?' asked Stephen.

'Always,' replied Antony. 'Openly. They wash all their clean linen in public.'

Love In A Spin (A Soap Opera)

BEFORE MAIN TITLE AND CREDITS INT. A LAUNDERETTE IN A CITY STREET. DAY.

POV THROUGH THE WINDOW OF A SPACE CAPSULE

as a mysterious object spirals round and round, filling the entire window. We hear futuristic space music as we watch the object spin. It looks like a bright nebula against a black background.

CAMERA BACK

to reveal that we have been watching an ultra-close up of clothes spinning in a washing machine in a launderette. The music changes to 'Wait Till You See Her' by Rodgers and Hart, played beautifully on a solo piano, over the MAIN TITLE, SUB-TITLE AND CREDITS.

In the launderette we see first MR PETTY, spruce, fussy, 50ish. He is very obviously trying to avoid contact with MRS MORONEY, shabby, sluttish, almost a 'bag lady', in her sixties. In charge at the launderette, giving change, doing service washes, getting machines to work, is LAURA, young, slim, beautiful. She does everything with calm efficiency and grace. The music fades.

EXT. THE STREET OUTSIDE THE LAUNDERETTE. DAY.

LUKE, young, pleasant-looking, is walking down the street. He is wearing a dark business suit and carrying a raincoat, briefcase, umbrella and magazine. He catches sight of a clock showing shortly before nine. He checks it against his watch: 8.49. He hurries his stride, late for work. But in front of the launderette he stops dead.

INT. THE LAUNDERETTE. DAY.

LUKE'S POV

of Laura as she works. Her body moves beautifully as she bends and shifts bags of washing. Her face is lovely as she soothes the complaining Mr Petty and smiles at Mrs Moroney.

EXT. THE STREET. DAY.

Luke is transfixed by Laura. After staring at her for a time (she does not notice) he pulls himself together and walks smartly away—in the opposite direction to his original walk.

INT. LUKE'S FLAT. DAY

Luke lets himself in. He hurls briefcase, magazine, umbrella and raincoat away from him. He reaches for the telephone and dials a local number.

LUKE

(into telephone)

Hello... Joyce?... Is Nose, er, Mr Parsons, there yet? It's Luke... Mr Marriott... Look, could you please tell him I'm very sorry I won't be in today, but the fact is I'm very ill? ...

As he speaks he removes his jacket and tie and then his shirt, revealing that he is very fit, almost aggressively healthy, just as he gets to the words 'very ill'.

While talking he lifts a weight with his spare hand.

LUKE (cont'd)

(still into telephone)

No, it was more like a dizzy spell. I thought I was seeing things and I could not move my feet... No, it came on very suddenly...

He rolls up his shirt and hurls it into a large plastic bag.

LUKE (cont'd)

(still into telephone)

Oh, thanks... Yes, I'll go straight to bed... No, I won't go out... Bye.

He hangs up. He paces energetically round the flat, grabbing towels and dirty clothes, anything that might be washed, and putting them into a plastic bag. He also grabs a big handful of change.

EXT. THE STREET. DAY.

Luke, now in casual clothes and training shoes, runs full tilt down the street, carrying the plastic bag of washing. He forces a car to brake abruptly with a SQUEAL: he does not notice. He vaults without breaking stride over some WORKMEN drinking tea by the side of a hole. A shirt falls from his bag. PEOPLE shout and point: he does not notice. He rushes into the launderette.

INT. THE LAUNDERETTE. DAY

Luke looks round for Laura. His face falls as there is no sign of her, only Mr Petty and Mrs Moroney.

Mr Petty fussily folds some items from his immaculate wash. Mrs Moroney lights an ill-rolled cigarette and takes something crumby and jammy from one of her bags. Laboriously and deliberately she walks over to Mr Petty and smokes and eats over his wash. With a tetchy gesture he withdraws it, just in time as Mrs Moroney drips crumbs, ash and jam.

LUKE

(still looking round)

Oh... I wanted a girl. I mean, is there someone in charge?

Mr Petty and Mrs Moroney stare at him. Laura returns from the small back room of the launderette.

LAURA

Can I help you?

LUKE

Oh. Yes. Very much.

But he has no idea what to say next as he looks at her.

LAURA

(smiling, and no trace of sarcasm)

This is a launderette.

She opens an empty washing machine and does an elaborate mime of loading it, followed by churning clothes.

LAURA (cont'd)

Do you speak English?

LUKE

Only if you're going to...

She turns away and at last he thinks of a question to ask her.

LUKE (cont'd)

How much is it?

LAURA

Eighty pence.

She gestures towards a very large sign saying 'Automatic Wash—80 pence' in his direct line of sight.

LUKE

Thank you. Thank you very much.

He starts to load his wash but still stares at her. She again turns away and heads for the back room.

LUKE (cont'd)

Wait!

She stops.

LAURA

Yes?

Luke pulls out a fistful of change. It contains many 10p pieces, which he hastily stuffs back into his pockets before she can see them.

LUKE

Have you any ten-pee pieces?

He trades a fifty-pee piece for five tens.

LUKE'S POV

of her hands as she gives him the change. No wedding ring or other jewellery.

LUKE (cont'd)

Thank you. Thank you very much.

He places 80p in the coin slot of the machine. He pushes in the coin-lever. After a pause she helps him. Their eyes meet for an instant, THE MACHINE STARTS. They watch Luke's clothes through the window.

LAURA

Would you like to go away and leave them?

LUKE

No!

LAURA

I could do them for you.

LUKE

I'm sure you're marvellous. But I'd rather stay.

SERIES OF SHOTS

as Laura moves around the launderette doing various tasks. Luke turns his back on his wash to watch her.

Mr Petty holds out one end of a large garishly patterned sheet.

MR PETTY

Miss? Miss?

Laura helps him fold the sheet. Their bodies almost touch.

ON LUKE

clenching his fists.

LUKE
(to himself)

You... animal!

Mrs Moroney, cigarette in mouth, walks laboriously and deliberately straight through the sheet which Laura and Mr Petty are folding, causing him to drop his end onto the floor. He retrieves it, tetchily. Mrs Moroney smiles faintly and continues her walk to the telephone at the end of the launderette.

MRS MORONEY

Time for me call.

Laura gives her a 10p piece for the telephone. Mrs Moroney dials, then inserts the coin.

MRS MORONEY (cont'd)
(into telephone)

Hello?... Evie?... How's the market this morning?...
You could get me some more coffee... and sugar...
But I don't want any more tins...

Laura approaches Luke. In the b.g. Mrs Moroney still talks.

LAURA

Laundry's finished.

LUKE

That's awful! Will you get another job?

LAURA

Yourlaundry's finished. Your machine stopped five minutes ago.

LUKE

I never noticed. Time flies when you're enjoying yourself.

LAURA

Would you like a spin?

LUKE

Only if you're having one.

LAURA

You could just have a tumble.

The thought of this makes him fall over into an empty laundry basket.

She smiles, nicely, and mimes as if to lift him into the tumble dryer. Back to her face as we DISSOLVE TO

EXT. THE STREET. DAY.

Luke emerges from the launderette with his plastic bag of washing. We hear a Beatles song: 'I've just seen a face I can't forget...' as Luke runs down the street doing tricks with the laundry bag, throwing it, catching it, dribbling it. He dropkicks it over the workmen, still drinking tea by the side of the hole, vaults over them again, and catches the bag on the other side of them.

INT. LUKE'S FLAT. DAY.

The Beatles song continues 'She's just the girl for me and I want all the world to see we've met...' as Luke lets himself in. He hurls the laundry bag away. Clothes cascade about him.

INT. THE 'GOOD HOPE' PUB. EVENING.

The Beatles song plays from the pub jukebox 'Falling... Yes, I am falling... and she keeps calling me back again...' as Luke strides into the pub and joins his friend ALBERT (business suit and distinctive shirt, slightly older) at the bar. The music fades.

ALBERT

I thought you were ill.

LUKE

I'm getting married.

ALBERT

It can be fatal. Look at my wife. On second thoughts...

A beat.

ALBERT (cont'd)

Who's the girl?

LUKE

I don't know.

ALBERT

You've no one specific in mind.

LUKE

She's very specific. I just don't know her name.

ALBERT

It's always nice to have something to discover on the honeymoon. What else don't you know about her?

LUKE

She's gentle. She's kind. She… gives change.

ALBERT

She's a golden-hearted tram conductor.

LUKE

She works in the launderette. God, I'd give her the shirt off my back.

ALBERT

That's what she's for. What does she look like?

Luke tries to answer but is stumped.

LUKE

For hell's sake, Albert, she was beautiful. How can I remember what she looked like?

ALBERT

But you would recognize her if you saw her again?

LUKE

I might never see her again. Unless… I must have laundry. Every day. Albert—I want your laundry.

ALBERT

Grace looks after it.

Luke falls to his knees.

LUKE

Please, Albert. Just a few samples. Bring them

into work tomorrow. I can do them in my lunch hour.

ALBERT

All right.

LUKE

Bless your cotton socks.

INT. THE LAUNDERETTE. DAY.

Laura is working in the launderette. There are more CUSTOMERS than before but they still include Mr Petty and Mrs Moroney.

From outside the launderette Luke watches Laura. He is carrying a plastic bag full of washing (Albert's—we can recognize his shirt from the evening before). Luke shuffles, almost walks away, then nerves himself to walk in.

LUKE

Hello. Isn't it a lovely day? Even better than yesterday.

He searches Laura's face for encouragement, but finds none in particular.

LUKE (cont'd)

Or perhaps you prefer yesterday?

He looks down, embarrassed, at his bag of washing.

LUKE (cont'd)

Ah. Yes. This. Do you know I had drinks with a friend last night and I wore one of the shirts I did here and he had to put on sunglasses.

Laura smiles.

LUKE (cont'd)

He begged me to do his for him, I mean it was embarrassing, he fell on his knees. So I'm back.

He has a sudden idea.

LUKE (cont'd)

I just thought, do they give you a commission on each wash that people bring in?

LAURA

What a good idea. But I'm afraid not.

LUKE

They couldn't afford it.

LAURA

Well, thank you. Do you want change?

LUKE

Is it still eighty?

LAURA

Yes.

LUKE

Astonishing. Such marvellous value.

LAURA

(looking daggers at Mr Petty)

Some people think it's a lot.

LUKE

It's not much to pay for one's Destiny.

Before Laura can react to this melodramatic remark there is a racking cough from Mrs Moroney.

MRS MORONEY

I need the phone again, dear.

Laura gives her 10p. Mrs Moroney heads for the phone. Yet again she disrupts Mr Petty's wash, and smiles faintly as she does. She dials and inserts 10p.

MRS MORONEY (cont'd)

(into telephone)

Hello, Evie?... You went?... They couldn't do them? Well, if they can't do them in the market you can get them on the curb...

LUKE'S WASHING MACHINE STARTS UP.

LUKE

There's something wonderfully exciting, isn't there about the start of a washing machine? Except that you must have heard it thousands of times.

LAURA

Oh no, I still love it.

LUKE

I mean, there's something
majestic about that first rush of water.

LAURA

(confidingly)

Whenever I see it I feel I'm in the secret cave of Neptune, God of the Sea.

LUKE

Oh absolutely.

A red light suddenly illuminates on his machine.

LUKE (cont'd)

Good grief, what's that red light?

LAURA

Oh, that's only if you want to add bleach.

LUKE

Do *you* add bleach?

LAURA

No.

LUKE

No, I don't either. It's awful stuff, bleach, don't you think? It just … bleaches everything. Still some people like it.

LAURA

I do sometimes use fabric conditioner.

LUKE

Oh, that's quite another thing, fabric conditioner. Great stuff, fabric conditioner, when you want to … condition fabrics.

LAURA

That's when I use it.

A long pause as Luke tries to follow up this promising exchange. Abruptly he holds out his right hand.

LUKE

Luke.

LAURA

(trying to follow where his right hand points)

Where?

LUKE

No, I mean Luke as in Luke my name. Luke Marriott.

LAURA

Laura.

They shake hands.

LUKE

My favourite name. Laura… what?

LAURA

(thinks for a moment, then, straight-faced)

Laura LenHARdy.

LUKE

Laura Len…

He holds up a dirty towel.

LUKE (cont'd)

Here's another fine mess.

LAURA

Really, Laura Caston.

LUKE

Is there a Mr Caston?

LAURA

There was.

LUKE

I'm sorry.

LAURA

I'm not.

A pause.

LUKE

Do you live near here?

LAURA

No, I live at Reppingham.

LUKE

That's miles.

LAURA

The 261 takes me all the way.

LUKE

I've never taken the 261. But a cousin of mine takes it all the time. Swears by it. I see the 261 sometimes from my flat.

A beat.

LUKE (cont'd)

You could see my flat…

He glances at her quickly but sees no encouragement.

LUKE (cont'd)

… from the 261 bus. If you sat on top. I could wave.

His machine has stopped.

LAURA

Your wash is over.

LUKE

Only the dryer to look forward to.

LAURA

I could give you extended time.

LUKE

Would you really?

LAURA

Don't tell Mr Petty, over there.

LUKE

Is there anyone else who gets extended time?

LAURA

That's my business.

LUKE

Sorry. That was out of order. But I can see you again?

LAURA

If you've got something to wash.

INT. ALBERT'S HOME. NIGHT.

Luke has just had dinner with Albert and his wife, GRACE (overdressed, shrill). The room contains a large sofa with a loose cover in a lurid floral design.

GRACE

Albert says you've become a dirty young man.

She laughs, explosively and horribly.

LUKE

It was even better than yesterday. We talked about so many things.

ALBERT

Like what?

LUKE

Bleach. We see bleach exactly the same way. And fabric conditioner. On fabric conditioner we're like twin souls.

GRACE

Do you think she could put some starch into Albert?

She laughs, as before.

LUKE

Do you know she catches the 261 bus?

GRACE

Albert couldn't catch flu, even when everybody was catching it.

She laughs, as before.

ALBERT

Now you know her name and she's not married now, but there could be somebody else?

LUKE

I've got to see her tomorrow. I can't wait till next week. I need your laundry again.

GRACE

You did it all today, Luke. We haven't got any more.

LUKE

Grace. My whole life depends on this. I must have some laundry.

ALBERT

We really have nothing left.

LUKE

The whole country is flooded with filth. How can you not have anything grubby?

On an inspiration Luke leaps up and seizes the lurid loose cover off the sofa.

LUKE (cont'd)

I'll wash this for you.

GRACE

But it's clean.

LUKE

Prevention is better than cure.

INT. THE LAUNDERETTE. DAY.

Laura is working in the launderette. Few customers, but they include Mr Petty and Moroney. Luke walks in with another bag full of wash. It is a beautiful sunny

LUKE

Filthy day!

LAURA

(surprised, gestures at sunshine)

It's lovely...

LUKE

Ever since I met you every day has been a filthy day. You've made me see things in a new way—dirty, mucky, sordid. You probably wonder why I'm here again.

LAURA

No.

LUKE

Can I trust you?

He pulls Grace's lurid sofa cover from his plastic bag. He uses it to form a screen around them.

LUKE (cont'd)

I'm an undercover agent. Under cover. From the FBI, the Filth Begone Institute. My job is to fight grime.

LAURA

So's mine. Eight service washes today. So no chat.

She bustles off, loading and unloading machines. Luke loads the sofa cover into his machine. His MACHINE STARTS. He watches Laura for a while. She is absorbed in her work, and ignores him. He leaves the launderette, waving as he goes.

INT. A NEWSAGENT'S SHOP. DAY.

A shop interior, selling newspapers and garish sweets. A middle-aged WOMAN serves behind the counter. Luke comes in and buys a newspaper. Then his eye is caught by the sweet display, especially a collection of marzipan crocodiles.

LUKE

How much are the crocodiles?

WOMAN

Five pence.

LUKE

Could I have ten, please?

She starts to pick up crocodiles, but he checks her.

LUKE (cont'd)

Do you mind? I'd like that one… and that one… not him, he's lost a leg, poor chap… that one… the red one… that fat one… Now, one more for luck.

She holds up crocodiles one by one for his inspection.

LUKE (cont'd)

Not that one... Not that one... Oh no...

As she holds up a particularly beautiful crocodile,

LUKE (cont'd)

I'll take that one.

WOMAN

I'm sorry, sir, that one's
reserved.

INT. THE LAUNDERETTE. DAY.

Laura is away in the back room. Mr Petty and Mrs Moroney are the only customers. Mr Petty, as usual, is making a big production of folding something. Mrs Moroney is smoking and eating, both sordidly.

The TELEPHONE rings. It is much nearer Mrs Moroney than Mr Petty but she ignores it. Mr Petty glares at her, hinting that she might pick it up, but she outfaces him. At last he gives way, drops his folding and answers the phone.

MR PETTY

(into telephone)

Yes?... Who?... Mrs
Moroney?...

In the most leisurely manner Mrs Moroney gets up and takes the phone from Mr Petty, who returns to his folding.

MRS MORONEY

(into telephone)

Just a minute, Evie...

She carries the earpiece, which has a very long cord, and deposits it right beside Mr Petty, where it begins to slide and swing about in an irritating way. Mrs Moroney walks straight past Mr Petty and takes a match from Laura in the back room. Mr Petty cannot bear the swinging telephone, and holds it still, thereby again being forced to drop his folding. Mrs Moroney returns and collects the instrument from him with no acknowledgement or thanks.

MRS MORONEY (cont'd)

(into telephone)

That's right, Evie, if they haven't got any wool,
the cotton's no good to me...

Luke returns, bearing an evening paper and a bag full of crocodiles.

LUKE
(to Laura)

Would you like to see?...

But before he can offer Laura the paper, Mrs Moroney claws it from him. She heads straight for one page and discards all the others on to the floor.

LUKE (cont'd)
(to Laura)

...a crocodile?

She smiles as he offers her a marzipan crocodile. They eat one apiece, then stage a mock fight between two others.

LUKE (cont'd)

Have you ever seen a real crocodile, in the wild?

LAURA

No.

LUKE

Neither have I.

A beat.

LUKE (cont'd)

Gives us something in common.

ON LAURA

as she makes her little crocodile turn away from him, and then matches the action herself.

Luke opens a washing machine which has stopped.

LUKE (cont'd)

Aaaagh!

He unfolds the sofa cover. It is the same colour but all the flowers have gone.

LUKE (cont'd)

I can't take this back. She'll kill me to death! I'd rather face nuclear piranha fish or Jeremy Paxman...

Calmly Laura returns and opens the next-door washing machine. She extracts Grace's sofa cover—spotlessly clean and perfectly florid.

LUKE (cont'd)

Saved!

INT. ALBERT'S HOUSE. NIGHT.

Luke is holding out the sofa cover for Grace and Albert to admire.

GRACE

Very nice...

Luke puts down the sofa cover.

LUKE

I have to see her again. Are you sure you have no more laundry?

GRACE

Not a stitch.

ALBERT

Luke, you can't go to the laundry every day.

LUKE

Why not? I love that laundry. I love to see her turning the world clean. Please give me something. I must go there tomorrow.

GRACE

Sorry...

Luke grabs the sofa cover back.

LUKE

I'll do this again.

GRACE

But it's just been washed.

LUKE

Well, don't let's leave everything to the last possible minute.

EXT. OUTSIDE ARTHUR'S HOUSE. NIGHT.

Albert is saying goodbye to Luke.

ALBERT

I'm sorry we couldn't give you back the sofa cover.

LUKE

All right, but please don't just sit on it.

ALBERT

We'll try to save you some things for next week.

LUKE

Thanks, but what about tomorrow?

INT. LUKE'S FLAT. NIGHT.

Luke prowls around searching for things to wash. The haul is meagre: two handkerchiefs and a very few items from his laundry basket. Everything else is spotless and he looks at it with despair. He takes out a clean shirt, hurls it on to the floor and walks all over it. He is about to repeat the process on another when he hears a CRACK OF THUNDER. He looks out and sees that it is pouring with rain, and his face lights up.

EXT. OUTSIDE LUKE'S FLAT. NIGHT.

Belting rain. Luke rushes out with an armful of clean clothes, which, delightedly, he hurls into the rain and the puddles.

LUKE

Blow winds and crack your cheeks! Rage!
You cataracts and hurricanoes spout
Till you have drenched our tea-towels,
Drowned our socks!...

Lights go on in neighbouring windows as Luke holds up a now filthy shirt to the moon.

INT. THE LAUNDERETTE. DAY.

Luke is washing the previous night's wash and talking to Laura. Mrs Moroney is the only other customer, on the telephone in the b.g.

LUKE

...there it was, the dog grabbed my clothes and
the next thing I knew they were all over the yard
in the rain. Would you believe it?

Laura's face suggests not.

LUKE (cont'd)

Amazing bit of luck, really. Croc?

He offers her a marzipan crocodile from a bag. She smiles and takes it.

Mr Petty bursts in, furious.

MR PETTY

My socks! I am missing a valuable pair of socks.

LAURA

I'll have a look for you.

She goes into the back room and returns with a bag full of lost property.

LAURA (cont'd)

What colour?

MR PETTY

Aquamarine and magenta. You must have them.

LAURA

Nothing like that here.

MR PETTY

Impossible. I'm calling the police.

LAURA

All right. I'm sure Mrs Moroney will give you the phone since it's such an emergency.

MR PETTY

Well, maybe not the police. But unless I receive full and adequate compensation I shall take my custom elsewhere in future.

LAURA

Oh, no, Mr Petty, please, I couldn't bear that. It's not your laundry I want, Mr Petty, it's you. Couldn't you sense my animal passion? Whenever I handled your underwear I thought of you inside it. When we folded sheets together I thought of us between them. Take me, Mr Petty. Give me your soap!

By now she has him in a passionate embrace. Luke watches in admiration and amazement. Mrs Moroney is still on the phone, ignoring the whole scene. The terrified Mr Petty breaks free and flees.

MRS MORONEY

(into telephone, but gazing at fleeing Petty)

Pork belly.

INT. LUKE'S OFFICE. DAY.

Luke is rehearsing an imitation of Mr Petty. There is a huge pile of work in his IN tray and none at all in his OUT tray. He looks at both trays for a moment and reverses the labels, then strides out, jauntily.

INT. THE LAUNDERETTE. DAY.

Laura is working. There are a number of CUSTOMERS but for once not Petty or Moroney. A VICAR comes in with a large bag. He is very furtive and anxious to conceal its contents. He tips the contents into a machine and says a short prayer in front of it. Time passes. The vicar continues to block the view of his wash. Other customers leave, but the vicar waits until he is alone with Laura before unguarding his machine.

LAURA

It's all right. They've gone.

At last the vicar reveals his wash. Not naughty underwear or women's clothing, as we have come to expect, but a large (wet) cuddly E T. He hurries away with it.

Luke bursts in, for once without a bag of washing.

LUKE

(as Mr Petty)

My socks! I am missing a valuable pair of socks.

LAURA

(apathetically)

What colour?

LUKE

Topaz and gamma-ray.

LAURA

We haven't got them.

LUKE

You've sold them! You and Petty are in this together. You've bootlegged my socks!

Laura does not join in the game.

LUKE (cont'd)

Unless I receive full and adequate compensation I shall take my custom elsewhere in future.

He waits for her to vamp him. No response.

LUKE (cont'd)

Aren't you going to try desperately to make me change my mind?

LAURA

No.

A beat.

LAURA

Sorry.

LUKE

I'm sorry. I wanted to come here, that's all. Look, I can take my custom elsewhere if you want.

LAURA

It's all right.

LUKE

If something has made you unhappy I wish… you'd let me wash it out for you.

He turns away and is about to leave.

LAURA

Thank you for all the crocodiles.

He smiles and waves, imitating snapping jaws.

LAURA (cont'd)

Have a dirty weekend.

SERIES OF SHOTS

of Luke's weekend.

EXT. A FOOTBALL PITCH. DAY.

Luke is goalkeeper. The pitch is wet and muddy. Luke brings off a flying save and then does a victory roll into the mud. His TEAM MATES applaud, ironically.

A TEAM MATE

Hang about, Luke, we haven't kicked off yet!

LUKE

Let's not leave everything to the last possible minute!

INT. A BAR. EVENING.

After the match Luke is showing off to his team, balancing a jug of beer on his head. He tries an ambitious stunt and beer cascades over his shirt.

INT. LUKE'S BEDROOM. DAY.

Luke has a huge messy breakfast alone in bed. Not satisfied with the results, he deliberately butters one of the sheets.

INT. LUKE'S FLAT. DAY.

Luke decants dirty football kit, shirt and sheets into his laundry bag. He tosses it in the air, pleased with its bulk.

INT. THE LAUNDERETTE. DAY.

Laura is working. Mrs Moroney is on the telephone. Luke enters bouncily with his bag.

MRS MORONEY
(into telephone)

You can tell them at that price—I should cocoa!

She hangs up and sweeps out of the launderette, ignoring Luke.

LUKE

Listen to this, listen to this... What's the best town in England to open a launderette?... Give up? Staines.

He laughs explosively; Laura finds herself joining in.

LUKE (cont'd)

Would you like to come out for a bite of lunch?

LAURA

I've got to run this place.

LUKE

You've only got one customer. I'm sure he won't mind.

But right on cue, in comes another customer, MICK, young, tall, flashily handsome, very powerfully built. He is arrogant, proprietorial, and knows himself to be irresistible to women.

MICK
(looking straight through Luke)

Hello, sweetheart. It's your favourite underwear.

LAURA

(tonelessly)

Have you got change? Or do you want me to do it for you?

MICK

Any time, darling, but I'll do my laundry.

He fills a washing machine and pushes in the coin lever in a coarse, suggestive way. He notices Luke for the first time.

MICK (cont'd)

Busy day, pal?

He looks hintingly at the door. Luke walks to the telephone and dials.

LUKE

(into telephone)

Joyce?… Luke. I'm not in this afternoon.

He hangs up and sits down, with a brief stare at Mick.

A long pause, as Luke and Mick try to outsit each other. Laura ignores both.

Mick gets up and struts over to a dryer. He takes off his sweater and a T-shirt beneath and throws them in, and starts the dryer. He admires his magnificent physique in the glass before returning to the bench and sprawling in front of Laura. She does not react. Luke seethes.

Laura goes into the back room and returns with a heavy bag of washing.

LUKE

Here, let me.

He takes the bag from her and juggles with it effortlessly, looking up to see if she is impressed.

She gives him no sign as she takes the bag and loads the wash into a machine. She puts a coin in the soap machine. It fails to deliver and she taps it.

LUKE (cont'd)

Here, let me.

He delivers the machine a smashing karate chop with a wild cry. Soap torrents out of it. He looks up, but she is not impressed. She puts some of the soap into the machine she has loaded.

A MACHINE STOPS. Laura has trouble opening it.

LUKE (cont'd)

Here, let me.

He kicks the handle. The machine flies open, but she is not impressed. She loads wash from it into a plastic basket but before she can pick up the basket

LUKE (cont'd)

Here, let me.

He picks up the basket, balances it on his head, and walks towards the dryers. She is not impressed.

Luke resumes his place and tries again to sit out Mick. Mick's DRYER STOPS and he very slowly extracts and puts on his warmed T-shirt and sweater, leering towards Laura.

MICK

Cor... great. Want me to do yours, doll?

Laura does not react. But behind his back Luke feeds a huge quantity of soap powder into Mick's washing machine. Mick sits down and combs and re-combs his hair.

Suddenly Mick's MACHINE CLANKS AND COUGHS and spurts foam.

MICK (cont'd)

Bloody hell! I got me flares in there.

Laura switches off the machine from the mains and prepares to mop up the engulfing foam. Luke strolls forward.

LUKE

Here, let me.

LAURA

NO! Out! Get out, both of you! Out!

They look amazed as she charges them with the mop.

LAURA (cont'd)

You heard me, out! Laundry's closed. I'll leave your washes in the café. Now, out!

She drives them both out with a manic mop.

INT. THE LAUNDERETTE. DAY.

Laura is working alone. The mess from Luke and Mick has been cleared. Luke walks in, nervously: no laundry bag, but he is carrying a paper one.

LUKE

I'm sorry about yesterday.

LAURA

You have to understand. I can't bear it if people try to take over this laundry. I love this laundry. I have nothing else. Nothing gets between me and this laundry.

LUKE

I'm sorry again. I don't have to come here. I came here today only to give you these.

He gives her his paper bag. She empties it. A cascade not only of marzipan crocodiles but other shapes—mice, monsters, teeth, cigars, fried eggs. She laughs.

LAURA

I'll never get through these—without help.

SERIES OF SHOTS

as Luke establishes a routine of assembling laundry and then visiting Laura. (Music: The Beatles 'There's A Place'). Each visit sees him jump over the same tea-drinking workmen in the hole in the road.

He resorts to more and more far-fetched methods of acquiring laundry, whether his own or other people's.

Again he raids his own flat for everything washable.

He plays strip poker with Albert and Grace, and puts their clothes in his laundry bag when he wins.

He goes to a charity shop and buys old clothes at random to put in his laundry bag.

He sits in a restaurant with bright fabric tablecloths and linen napkins. He gives an order to a WAITER, who returns bringing cloth and napkins instead of food.

He prowls around outside the launderette. An ELDERLY MAN struggles by with a laundry bag. Luke stops him and buys the laundry bag for a generous sum in notes.

As soon as he has acquired some laundry Luke goes to the launderette. He talks with Laura and buys them more crocodiles. Sometimes he gestures as if inviting her to step outside, but each time she smiles, shakes her head and retreats to do a job in the launderette. Mrs Moroney is often there. She looks ever more shabby and downtrodden. She is constantly on the phone. Laura gives her change and cups of tea.

INT. THE GOOD HOPE PUB. EVENING.

Luke joins Albert at the bar and gives him a bag of washing.

Thanks. How much do I owe you?

LUKE

This one's on me.

ALBERT

They've all been on you. How's it going?

LUKE

She still won't come out with me. Well, why should she? To her I'm just… dirt.

ALBERT

You'll have to do something to impress her.

LUKE

I tried that and she charged me with a mop.

ALBERT

How much did she charge you? No, I mean, you have to show her you're someone special and memorable. That's what I did for Grace. Special and memorable.

LUKE

How did you do that for Grace?

ALBERT

I can't remember.

INT. THE LAUNDERETTE. DAY.

Laura at work, Mrs Moroney on the telephone. Luke enters with his laundry bag.

MRS MORONEY

(into telephone)

How much more do they want from me?… I tell you I've had my fill of them coppers!

She has a paroxysm of coughing and hangs up.

LAURA

Why don't you go home, Mrs Moroney? I'm sure

you'll feel better. Don't worry, it'll all come out in the wash.

She helps Mrs Moroney into the street, then returns.

LUKE

I think it's wonderful the way you look after that poor old lady.

Laura tries to say something but he rattles on.

LUKE (cont'd)

She's got nothing to wash, she just comes here for a bit of warmth. She can't get about to do her shopping, she has to ask someone over the phone to do it for her. Now she's in trouble with the police, you heard her...

Laura jams a crocodile into his mouth.

LAURA

I look after her because she is my boss. Mrs Moroney owns this launderette. She owns this whole street and about thirty others. She dresses as she does because she's so rich she can afford to and not care. Mrs Moroney uses my phone because she is afraid that hers is tapped, and that might lose her a lot of money. You see, when she phones from here she isn't shopping for groceries. She phones her broker in the City and she puts huge sums of money into the commodity futures market.

LUKE

Commodities?

LAURA

Yes. Commodities. Things like coffee. sugar tin... wool... cotton... pork belly... cocoa... copper... They each have a market. People make and lose millions in less than a minute. Mrs Moroney plays them all.

LUKE

Good grief.

LAURA

Actually I'd try to look after Mrs Moroney even if she wasn't the boss. I like her. I trust her. She's always right about people.

Luke takes in this last remark.

INT. LUKE'S OFFICE. DAY.

Luke is intently reading the Financial Times.

LUKE'S POV

of the page that grips him. It is of course the Commodities page. He looks up from time to time and mouths words, as if trying to memorize them.

LUKE

'Coffee: after a higher than expected opening in Robustas sellers appeared somewhat reluctant to short the market'... Special and memorable.

INT. THE LAUNDERETTE. DAY.

Laura is working. Luke strides in with his laundry bag. They share a crocodile and load his wash. Mrs Moroney shuffles in. Luke darts in front of her to the phone. He dials but screens the digits.

LUKE

(into telephone)

Fred? Sorry, I couldn't get you earlier... Look, about our project in the markets... the way I see it, copper has a firmer tone and I think we're looking at a three-month high of 1144... zinc standard I expect to be idle... Lead? Oh, barely steady...

Mrs Moroney makes efforts to grab the phone but he hangs on and cuts her out.

LUKE (cont'd)

(into telephone)

As to coffee, I feel that after a higher than expected opening in Robustas sellers might have been somewhat reluctant to short the market...

He looks round to Mrs Moroney for approval. She continues to clutch for the phone. He blocks her again.

LUKE (cont'd)

(into telephone)

The market has already discounted the American election, don't you think, Fred?... I think we need a position against 1992...

A beat.

LUKE (cont'd)

Yes, but let's not leave everything to the last possible minute!

Mrs Moroney pulls a faint. Luke drops the phone and rushes to help her, as does Laura. Mrs Moroney recovers at once, grabs the phone, listens to it, then holds it out with a faint smile.

The VOICE can be heard at the other end of the line. It is the SPEAKING CLOCK: 'At the third stroke, it will be 12.32 precisely.'

ON LUKE

caught out, embarrassed, humiliated. Not special and memorable.

INT. THE LAUNDERETTE. DAY.

Laura and Luke are alone.

LUKE

I'm sorry about the phone call. I thought, if she listened... Well, it doesn't matter now. It was just a stunt. The whole thing's been just a stunt, my coming here, a stunt that didn't come off. Anyway, goodbye. I won't be back. I'll always remember this as a wonderful launderette.

He heads for the door.

LAURA

Wait!

He stops, with a faint hope that she cares for him.

LAURA (cont'd)

You've forgotten your laundry.

Hope abandoned.

LUKE

I'd like you to keep it.

EXT. THE STREET OUTSIDE THE LAUNDERETTE. EVENING.

For the first time we see the street in the evening. It looks melancholy and romantic. So does Luke, gazing out of the shadows. A cat miaows. Suddenly (and exactly like Orson Welles in The Third Man) Luke is illuminated by a light from a window above him.

LUKE'S POV

of the launderette and Laura working in it. She sees off the last CUSTOMERS (not Mrs Moroney) and switches off machines and lights.

Luke back out of the light and she comes out and locks the launderette. She walks down the street. He forces himself not to move. He even takes a pace or two in the opposite direction. It is impossible: he turns back and watches her again.

She quickens her pace. He looks round for the reason and sees behind him a distant 261 bus heading for Reppingham.

She starts to run. He turns and runs after her, but ducking and weaving into the shadows. He vaults over the same hole in the road which was there at the start: no workmen in it this time, but a pile of stuff for making tea.

The bus overtakes Luke. Laura sees it gaining on her; she runs faster. Luke sees this and abandons all attempts at concealment. He runs flat out, arms pumping.

The bus overtakes Laura. She runs faster.

Luke runs even faster. He encounters a PASSER-BY swinging a rolled umbrella. Arms still pumping, Luke grabs the umbrella without breaking stride, like a baton in a relay race.

ON THE PASSER-BY

as he does a double take. This reveals him to be ALFRED HITCHCOCK. Luke ignores him and runs on.

The bus makes it to the bus stop, which is empty. THE CONDUCTOR leans out, sees Laura running for the bus, waits till she has all but made it, then RINGS HIS BELL. The bus moves off without her.

Luke sees this and stops running. He walks slowly towards Laura, still carrying 'Hitchcock's' umbrella. Laura has her back to him as she stares furiously at the receding bus.

LUKE

Hello.

She gives a start, then relaxes when she sees who it is.

LUKE (cont'd)

I've brought you an umbrella.

LAURA

But it's not raining.

LUKE

Let's not leave everything to the last possible minute.

She smiles.

LUKE (cont'd)

It wasn't much of a goodbye this afternoon. I want to say goodbye properly. Or at least that you're the most wonderful person I've ever met. Look, it's a long time to your next bus. My flat is right here and it's warmer than outside. I won't try any stunts, promise. If I do you can scream the house down, it's jerry built.

LAURA

All right.

INT. LUKE'S FLAT. EVENING.

Luke takes Laura through the hall into his living room and switches on the lights.

She gasps.

LAURA

Everything's so clean.

Indeed it is. Everything which could be washed has been to the launderette, many times.

LAURA (cont'd)

I love things to be clean. That's why I work in a launderette. I used to work in an office. It was horrid. Lots of files with dust on them. And that awful carbon paper, it put smudges on all my clothes...

She shudders at the memory and bursts into tears. Sympathetically, Luke hands her a spotless anti-macassar and she dabs her face with it.

LAURA (cont'd)

Can I see everything?

They go through Luke's flat. In each room she is interested only in things which have been to the wash. Sometimes she picks them up and caresses them. There is no hint of the erotic in her gestures; she is simply a connoisseur of fine washing. They end up in the kitchen, where she opens a door leading apparently to a cupboard or a small utility room.

LAURA (cont'd)
(astonishment and delight)

Oh my God!

LAURA'S POV

of a fantastic, computerized, hypermodern, utterly automated washing machine. She runs her hands all over it, in homage and awe.

LAURA (cont'd)

Does it work?

LUKE

Perfectly.

She takes this in.

LAURA

But you've been coming to the launderette every day for weeks—even in the rain. Why?

LUKE

Surely you know?

LAURA

But you never told me... I never realized... You gave up this to see me?

He nods.

LAURA (cont'd)

I've always dreamed of using a machine like this.

LUKE

Please. Be my guest.

But he looks round, sadly.

LUKE (cont'd)

But there's nothing to wash.

LAURA

Oh yes there is.

INT. LUKE'S KITCHEN. NIGHT.

A very dim light (with occasional flickers of red and green) reveals Laura and Luke propped up on cushions on the kitchen floor. They are both totally nude, locked in each other, and ecstatically happy. They are not gazing, as might be expected, into each other's eyes. Instead, together, they watch Luke's marvellous machine washing their clothes (to the strains of Ravel's Bolero).

Last Over

'They lived happily and spotlessly ever after,' said Antony. 'They got married almost at once. Mrs Moroney gave them the laundry as a wedding present, which was just as well for Luke, since he had got sacked from his job for persistent absenteeism. They prospered and now they own about a dozen more, all over the country. I can tell you that their laundry business has an excellent balance sheet... *balance sheet ... oh yes...'*

Luke Marriott's left hand was still so swollen that he could not get a glove on it. He gripped the bat awkwardly, both hands behind the handle, and braced himself to receive the last three balls of the over from Jess McFarland, fast, with the Spot to help him. He was forced to play the first, and the jar made him wring his bad hand. The second was wide of off stump. The third he bravely glanced to fine leg for two. The Frenetics needed 12 to win, one wicket left, two overs to go. Joel Hegarty survived a confident lbw appeal and was badly dropped at the wicket. He then produced one of his best shots, a back-foot drive. The four left the Frenetics 8 to win off nine balls. Joel was forced to block the next two. Frank Wall rearranged his field to deny Joel any rational single (knowing he could do nothing about Joel's irrational singles). Nat McFarland's final ball was an out-swinger far too good for Joel to touch. So Luke Marriott had to face the last over from Jess.

He blocked the first, again wincing with pain. The second beat him, missed the stumps, and was taken by the redfaced wicketkeeper standing back. Joel ran for the bat-ting end the moment he saw Luke miss it and made his ground comfortably. Luke sprinted to the other end: there was nothing wrong with his legs. The stolen bye left seven to win off four balls and brought the uninjured batsman to face.

Frank Wall moved the field to offer Joel a single. He refused, loudly. The fourth ball of the over travelled wide down the leg side and the redfaced wicketkeeper did well to prevent byes. Still seven to win, two balls left. Jess McFarland bowled a good length straight ball. Joel tried out his leg glance. The ball took a leading edge and lobbed towards mid-wicket.

'Catch it, Roy!' shouted Custer stupidly from extra cover. Unnerved, young Roy not only missed the catch but misfielded along the ground. 'Two!' bawled Joel and young Roy completed his own misery with a bad throw. The batsmen made the second easily. Five to win off the last ball.

Joel closed his eyes and performed a long calculation. It revealed that he had to hit a six to win. He performed another calculation and decided that of all his favourite strokes the straight drive over the bowler's head was most likely to achieve it. Frank Wall made an identical calculation and posted a long-on and a long-off. Joel saw them and re-calculated. The last ball was again straight and good length, and Joel decided to swing it over square leg.

The top edge flew high over the wicketkeeper. At deep fine leg Nat McFarland saw it late and had to fling himself wide and low for the catch. He got one hand to it but dropped it when his elbow hit the ground. 'Yes!' called Luke.

The batsmen completed two. In pain and self-disgust Nat had forgotten that the batsmen were allowed to run off a dropped catch. Frank Wall shouted at him: another run was completed as he picked up the ball to throw.

'Another!' called Joel and hared for the batting end.

The throw was fierce and straight but bounced badly in front of the stumps. The wicketkeeper failed to gather it and midwicket had to back up. The batsmen completed the fourth. 'Yes!' shouted Joel.

Young Roy kept his nerve. He lobbed the ball back to the wicketkeeper and gave him time to run out Luke by five yards.

It was a tie. The first in Frenetic history, Antony informed everyone.

No one left the Bat and Ball early that night. There were many verbal replays of the match. Almost everyone had an Excellent Moment to recall and many were forced to buy a jug (lemonade for drivers: Upton Cerney was a caring village). Stephen took names and addresses for prints of his photographs. Frank Wall led everyone into the pub garden and the townees were thrashed at Aunt Sally.

At last the Frenetics disappeared home. Antony offered Stephen a lift back to London with Pat Hobby. Pat recited the plot of the screenplay he had offered to Arthur Fraser, but Stephen fell asleep long before the first death.

Pat was safely delivered and Antony took Stephen back to his hotel. He accepted the offer of a nightcap, and discussed plans for Stephen's next travel book, in Borneo.

As Antony prepared to leave, Stephen said 'You were right about the Frenetics. They have all got something... out of the ordinary. But there's one missing.'

'What's that?'

'You told me the story of ten of the Frenetics and I have guessed the Bramleys' story. But I don't know *your* story.'

'But you do. I told you when we met. My name is my story. All my life I've just been the scorer. There's nothing at all interesting about me.'

Final Score

'Antony Arkwright Scorer, you have pleaded guilty to six specimen charges of fraud and false accounting. Behind them lies the creation of one of the most ingenious and well-executed frauds of modern times.

'You established a network of companies which purported to represent a substantial trading empire. The accounts of these companies were precise and meticulous: their books were works of art. Or perhaps I should say, works of artifice? They were good enough to deceive major banks and financial institutions in this country, in the United States and in Switzerland. None suspected at any time that the assets and profits of the companies at the heart of your empire were non-existent. You were able to use them as security for loans to acquire and manage companies with real and substantial assets.

'You might well have escaped detection for many more years, but for the letter which you addressed to Mr Stephen Devane, the author of several travel books. This letter, which has been exhibited to this court, set out precisely the detail of your criminal enterprise: unfortunately for you it never reached Mr Devane in Borneo but instead was delivered to the British Vice Consul, Mr Robinson, who rightly sent it to the Serious Fraud Office.

'In passing sentence I shall bear in mind that, by design, your victims included no private investors, only banks and financial institutions. I note too that you derived little or no personal profit from your deceits.

'In your letter to Mr Devane, and subsequently to this court, it was suggested that your prime motive for your criminal enterprise was to satisfy a kind of artistic longing. The court has heard expert testimony as to the effect of your childhood experience over your name, although I must say that many men with names far more unfortunate than yours have managed to endure life without resorting to crime.

'The considerable profits of your enterprise were used, it appears, largely to assist your friends in the Frenetic Cricket Club. Even your legal work was done by Mrs Harper, without revealing to her the fraud at its core. You arranged for Mr Wyatt to be offered a job in Brazil. You backed the play which brought Miss Sheila Fereday, Mrs Bramley, back to the stage, and that, at least, you are entitled to consider a public benefaction. When the laundry business of Mr and Mrs Marriott hit financial difficulties you arranged an injection of funds. You gave similar help to Mr Shaw. You saved Mr Hegarty from an unwise speculation.

'You were behind the rescue of Megalopolitan Television from a hostile takeover. You paid Tim Morrow's school fees, in secret. Finally, you set up a film production company, for no other purpose but to purchase an option on a screenplay by Mr Barnes and another on a virtually identical screenplay by Mr Hobby.

'With the exception of Mrs Harper, none of your friends ever knew that they were under any obligation to you. Throughout this time you continued to act as scorer for the Frenetic Cricket Club, as you put it in your letter to Mr Devane, "anonymous, invisible, recorder of the deeds of others." '

Stephen put down the transcript of the judge's remarks on sentence. He had an appointment at Brixhaven Open Prison. He had received a new commission from his publisher: not, for once, a travel book, but the authorized biography of Antony Scorer.